HILLS END

There was no indication on that sun-drenched morning that the little Australian timber town of Hills End was doomed. Yet while most of its people were on a picnic and seven of its children were searching nearby caves for aboriginal drawings the sky 'became glazed over with a bronze sheen', a cloud 'reached out of the north like a black arm and closed its hand round the sun', and the dark waters of the river flooded over the rock span between town and hills.

When the children had struggled back to Hills End they found it deserted and destroyed. Surrounded by wild mountain and forest country, threatened by a flooded river, an escaped bull, and shortage of food, they were faced with the problem of survival till help came.

None of the children were heroes, none of them were saints, all of them found that 'one didn't realize how wonderful parents were till they weren't there'. Yet they survived, partly by drawing on strength they had not known they possessed and partly by the determination of the last boy anyone would have suspected of having the qualities of a leader.

This is an absolutely riveting story, full of suspense, which will appeal to older readers.

Ivan Southall was born in 1921. He was sixteen when his first article was accepted by the *Melbourne Herald*. He then wrote thirty stories and articles which were published all over Australia. He served with the R.A.A.F. for five and a half years during the Second World War, and was awarded the D.F.C. in 1944. Ivan Southall has written many exciting books, and his work has been translated into seventeen languages. He lived for many years in Victoria, but is now resident in Sydney.

Some other books by Ivan Southall

ASH ROAD
TO THE WILD SKY
LET THE BALLOON GO
FINN'S FOLLY
JOSH

IVAN SOUTHALL

HILLS END

Illustrated by Jim Phillips

PUFFIN BOOKS

PUFFIN BOOKS

Published by the Penguin Group
Penguin Books Ltd, 27 Wrights Lane, London W8 5TZ, England
Viking Penguin, a division of Penguin Books USA Inc.
375 Hudson Street, New York, New York 10014, USA
Penguin Books Australia Ltd, Ringwood, Victoria, Australia
Penguin Books Canada Ltd, 2801 John Street, Markham, Ontario, Canada L3R 1B4
Penguin Books (NZ) Ltd, 182–190 Wairau Road, Auckland 10, New Zealand

Penguin Books Ltd, Registered Offices: Harmondsworth, Middlesex, England

First published by Angus & Robertson 1962
Published in Puffin Books 1965
19 20 18

Printed and bound in Great Britain by
Cox & Wyman Ltd, Reading
Set in Monotype Bembo

CONTENTS

A NOTE FROM THE AUTHOR

WHEN we came to live in this corner of the hills, years ago, everything was so beautifully quiet. It has livened up a little since then. Whether we should thank the children, or blame them, I'm not prepared to say. We brought Drew with us, of course, and soon Robbie arrived and, more recently, Elizabeth and Melissa. Other families have grown up round us, too.

Norma and Margaret's father is a farmer. Sandra and Phillip also live on the land. Gary and Rhonda send their hardy dad off to the city every day where he makes aeroplanes. Gail, Barbara, and Barry live a mile down the road near the Bald Hills and their father works at the timber mill – when he's not beating me at chess.

There are other children, naturally, but if I mentioned them all I'd fill the page. They're all part of this big family we have here, tucked away from the city's clamour, and for every one of them I have written this book. I believe I have been promising to do it for years. Just one thing, don't go imagining that it's written *about* you – well, not all of it – perhaps a little here and a little there, but only the good parts, of course.

IVAN SOUTHALL

CHAPTER ONE

Hills End

THERE was no indication that Saturday morning that the little town of Hills End was doomed. The day even began beneath a hot and cloudless sky to the delight of Miss Elaine Godwin, the schoolmistress. Miss Godwin loved these mountains so much that she had scorned all promotion and all thought of transfer to a less remote community. She had remained at Hills End year after year with never more than three dozen pupils to teach.

She had set her alarm for half past six, that being early enough for her purpose, but she was out of bed before it rang. The morning heat and the excitement of the day ahead made it impossible for her to rest any longer. A few minutes before six she was kindling her kitchen stove, tidying away the books she had browsed through the night before, sweeping out the daily accumulation of dust, and then walking briskly down to the box nailed to the tree beside the track.

As usual, her morning milk was waiting for her – one generous pint – in the same enamelled billy-can that she had placed there almost every evening for nine years.

Below her, along the hillside and down to the fringe of the river flats, smoke was beginning to rise vertically from one chimney after another. How calm this morning was, and how beautiful. And how strangely moving, because this for Hills End was the most exciting day of the year.

Little Harvey Collins – he had always been known as little Harvey (with a small 'l') – had been awake since half past four.

That was Harvey all over. Everything had to be done to the extreme. When he was naughty no one could be naughtier. When he fought no one could fight harder. And when he was good he was so, so good that everyone started getting nervous. His mother would lock up the china and his father would break into a sweat.

At half past four Harvey had roved through the house, stumbling into doors, tripping over rugs, and disturbing everyone and being roundly abused for his trouble.

'Harvey! For mercy's sake switch off that light and go back to bed.'

'Harvey! Is that the cupboard door? Close it at once. If you eat the lunches now they won't be cut again.'

'Harvey! If you dare touch that pie in the refrigerator I'll scalp you. It's for tomorrow's dinner. Go back to bed!'

He had gone back to bed, grumbling and mumbling and nibbling at miserable old biscuits and a big apple and as wide awake as he could have been.

The sun had come up and he had dressed and had crept out to the back step and had sat there with his arm round Buzz, his dog, waiting impatiently for that houseful of lazy people to get out of bed.

Next door, beyond the stout electric fence, he could see Rickard's cows wandering down to the milking shed, and still lower, along the track towards the distant house, Mr Rickard plodded home with his horse and cart after the milk round. Swinging from the axle, back and forth, was the hurricane lamp, still alight, and trotting behind as always was the old red collie dog.

Harvey sighed a deep, deep sigh of frustration and shifted himself to his swing and rocked backwards and forwards and saw that even the McLeods were up. Their house was down on the flats and Harvey could see the smoke from the chimney standing up like a pillar through the trees.

The McLeod children filled the house with chatter and laughter and excited squeals, and it was the responsibility of Frances, the eldest, to escort the younger ones to the bathroom to make sure they brushed their teeth and washed their faces and took the soap out of the water. To make sure that all the towels were hung back neatly on the rail, and that the taps were not dripping and that soap puddles were not everywhere over the floor. And then back to the bedrooms to ensure that they were all correctly dressed, with their underwear on and not left in the drawer, with all buttons done up, socks right side out, shoes on the proper feet and laced and polished, and hair brushed until it shone.

Frances handled them all more efficiently than her mother could have done. Her mother tired easily and lost her temper readily, but Frances was as patient as the day was long, always kindly, always firm, never seemed to be tired and very rarely lost her temper. Her mother couldn't imagine what she would do without her. She was so proud of Frances that there wasn't a soul in Hills End who didn't know about it. It was a miracle that any of the grown-ups liked Frances at all, because so often they had to listen to her mother's praises of her. It was Frances this, and Frances that. It was a wonder the girl didn't wear a halo.

Of course, Frances was excited, too. For all her adult way she was still a schoolgirl. She was as impatient as the rest of them, as eager as the rest of them and as bright-eyed as the rest of them. She dressed in her prettiest frock and smiled at her reflection in the mirror.

'Frances,' she said to herself, 'what a wonderful, wonderful day! Perhaps if I'm clever enough I might even be lucky enough to sit next to Paul Mace before he can move away.'

'Paul!'

'Yes, dad.'

'Will you please find your sister and bring her to the breakfast-table. If she wants to get out she's got to hurry herself.'

'Yes, dad.'

'Your mother is getting impatient and once she gets impatient everything goes to pieces. If your mother starts it'll ruin the day for us. I'll never forget last year as long as I live. If that happens again, I'll – I'll – '

'Yes, dad.'

Paul tramped into the wild garden because he knew that Gussie would be there somewhere, digging for crickets, or turning over leaves in search of caterpillars, or climbing tall trees to pet the baby birds.

'Guss-seeee!'

An untidy and pretty little head bobbed up from the grass. 'Do you want me?'

'Of course I don't want you,' snorted Paul. 'What would I want you for? But dad wants you and mum's getting impatient. Breakfast's on the table.'

'*Really* on the table?'

'Yes.'

Gussie sighed. 'Parents! Every time we go anywhere it's

always the same. Hurry, hurry, hurry. Bustle, bustle, bustle. Everyone gets nasty and short-tempered. I've been ready for hours. Hours and hours. Mum sent me outside because I was getting in the way.'

'Come on, come on!'

Gussie came, brushing the grass from her dress and the dust from her hands. 'Bah,' she said, 'parents chewing on the wood today of all days!'

Big timber was the life in the veins of Hills End. It was a robust little place full of strong men and brave women, and there were more trees in the mountains than they could ever use and the forest seemed to grow again almost as quickly as they cut it down. Ben Fiddler, the timber-mill boss, valued his axemen, his mill-hands, and his drivers, and treated them well. He knew how hard it was to bring new men in and to hold them. Hills End was a long, long way from the nearest town, and if the timber had not been of such rare quality and so highly valued on the markets of the world he never would have established his industry in the first place.

Eighty-five miles it was, across the mountains, from Hills End to the town of Stanley, over a dangerous road, never properly formed, yet used for nine months of the year by the heavy jinkers that carried the dressed logs to the mills and the wharves of the big city another two hundred miles farther on. The drivers knew the road and were ever careful, but even they would not venture over it once the rains began. Sometimes for two months, sometimes for three months of every year, Hills End was cut off from the world, except for the occasional hardy or eccentric bush-walker, and the mailman, arriving once a week in his jeep, nerve-racked and mud-splashed, always vowing that he would never make the trip again.

Added to the hazard of the road was the bridge at Fiddler's

Crossing, fifteen miles to the south of the hamlet. It spanned a frightening gorge cut to an immense depth by a thundering mountain torrent, the River Magnus. But for the bridge the gorge would be impassable. The mailman was always terrified that he would return to the bridge and find it down, and the mere thought of spending the rest of the wet in Hills End was, he said, 'enough to send any sane man screaming up the wall'.

Hills End might have been cut off in the wet season, but it wasn't idle. The axemen continued to fell the trees when the weather was fine enough; some logs dragged out by the bulldozers even reached the hamlet in the valley and were milled for the next carting season; other machinery was rested and overhauled; and many of the townspeople, knowing almost to the day when the wet would begin, moved out ahead of it to visit families and distant friends or take a holiday at the seaside.

Life might have been hard in some ways at Hills End, but the people were not poor, or unhappy, or without the better things of life. Their homes were comfortable, and their community shop was well stocked. They attended a social get-together on Friday nights, a film show on Saturday nights, and chapel on Sunday mornings (all in the one building) when Ben Fiddler took the pulpit and usually preached on the sins of city life.

Over the period of ten years which marked its whole history, Hills End had settled into a comfortable little rut. The people were content, there never had been a theft or a crime of violence, never a really serious accident, and nothing remotely resembling a disaster.

At seven o'clock on that fateful Saturday, Miss Elaine Godwin, the schoolmistress, put out a saucer of milk for her cat in the shade of her hydrangeas, shut her cottage door – but didn't lock it because no one turned a key in Hills End – slung her haversack, took up her long and knotted walking-stick, and turned down the track to the schoolhouse.

The hamlet lay beneath her, not far away, and smoke from the morning fires now drifted across the flats until it vanished in the vapour haze over the great River Magnus. The Magnus poured from the mountains, fed by a thousand springs and streams, rushed onwards over the rocks to the north, through the gullies and the gorges, on towards the distant plains.

When the mill was silent, except for the slow beat of the big diesel engine that generated light and power for Hills End, a keen ear could hear the river talking to itself, sometimes sighing, sometimes chuckling, sometimes growling, and occasionally crying out in warning. It was a peculiar thing about the Magnus – before rain it always began to rise. Those hundreds of little springs throughout the mountains began to run faster and the river opened its throat and stretched itself.

No one in Hills End, that morning, seemed to have noticed that the Magnus was restless and strangely swollen. It wasn't the wet season. This was the dry and dusty season anyway, it was Picnic Day, and Hills End was too full of the voices of children and their parents.

Before she had reached the bottom of her track, Miss Godwin could see the cars and the trucks lined up outside the hall. She could distinguish the McLeod children and the Buchanans, and even Ben Fiddler and his foreman, Frank Tobias, full of good humour, lifting the children on to the backs of the trucks and helping the womenfolk into the cabins. Almost the entire population of Hills End was already bustling round the hall or standing in family groups waiting for their particular call to board the car or the truck allotted to them. In another fifteen minutes the township would be empty and the long and exciting drive to the annual picnic races at Stanley would have begun. But it wouldn't have begun for Miss Godwin. She was not going.

She paused at the foot of her track and leant on her tall walking-stick and smiled over this little township of hers. She loved it and its people so much. She loved its simple houses, its smells, its sounds, and its untidiness. Its straggly growth had offended some people, but Miss Godwin was not the type of person or the type of teacher who expected everyone, always, to be spick and span and on their best behaviour. She knew it was hard for boys to wash behind the ears and for growing girls to be gentle and ladylike. She knew it was difficult for men to control their gardens when there were no fences, and that it was almost impossible for women to keep their houses clean when all the roads and tracks were cut up by bulldozers and tractors and timber jinkers, and when every passing vehicle raised a cloud of dust. She liked people to be natural. She'd rather have them happy and carefree than frightened of a little healthy untidiness.

She did like people to be happy, as they were now. She realized that in some ways she was a very lonely person. She had been a school-teacher for so long, working with children, that she simply wasn't relaxed in the company of adults. She sought her pleasure in the beauty of the earth, learning its story in the rocks and the plants and the tiny creatures she found along the river bank or in the mountains. Miss Godwin was writing a book about the mountains. She had been writing it for years. She knew every word of it by heart and was sure that some day it would make her famous. Miss Godwin didn't know that it was as dry as the dust at her feet.

Paul wasn't sure how it happened, but he found himself talking to Frances. Normally, he wouldn't have been seen dead talking to Frances, or to any other girl, for Paul, dapper fellow of thirteen that he was, was one hundred per cent boy. All girls were considered by him to be sub-human, a peculiar form of animal life that messed up an otherwise agreeable world. The most striking example, of course, was Gussie, that younger sister of his. He lumped all girls together in a group with Gussie. Girls were a pain in the neck.

So, that he should have been talking to Frances was a distinctly unusual event. Frances, though a born lady, had placed herself well.

'What,' she heard Paul say, 'is Miss Godwin doing up there?'

'Watching us go, I suppose.'

'Even I can see that,' he snorted, 'but everyone's going to the picnic this year.'

'Mr Tobias isn't.'

'Well, someone's got to stop at the mill. That always happens, and it's Mr Tobias's turn this year. I reckon we ought to make her go with us.'

Frances smiled. She wasn't really a child. 'You couldn't make Miss Godwin do anything. She's going up to the cave that Adrian found, the cave with the pictures in it. She's been dying to get up there.'

Paul made a noise that was probably a grunt. 'Pictures! Adrian tells so many whoppers. It's a story he made up to get himself out of trouble. He was away all day and he had to think of something or he would have got a hiding. It was the first thing that came into his head.'

'I believed him,' said Frances. 'And so did Miss Godwin.'

'Well, I've been to those caves a dozen times and I've never seen any aboriginal drawings – hands and devil men and snakes and things. Phooey! And it's pretty hard getting up there. Miss Godwin probably won't be able to do it without someone to show her the way, and then it'll be for nothing.'

'Why don't *you* show her the way?'

Paul stared at Frances. 'Don't be silly. It's Picnic Day.'

'So you're not worried then, are you?' said Frances.

'But I am. Miss Godwin's a good sport. It'd be awful if anything happened to her. Are you sure that's where she's going?'

'Of course I'm sure. She was telling us about it yesterday in history period. You were there.'

'I wasn't,' said Paul. 'I was up at her cottage splitting firewood . . . By golly, if this is another of Adrian's whoppers and if anything happens to Miss Godwin – '

Paul went looking for Adrian, and Frances, with a hand to the tail of the truck she was about to board, was suddenly unhappy. She respected Paul and she liked him much more than any other boy, and Frances would be content to wait for years and years – as she would have to do – until Paul realized she was waiting. Suddenly, she didn't want to get on the truck, not until she knew that Paul had forgotten that silly thing she had said – 'Why don't *you* show Miss Godwin the way?' She shouldn't have said it. The climb to the caves was dangerous, she felt sure, and she didn't want Paul in danger any more than she wanted Miss Godwin in danger.

Adrian was already installed in the first truck, best seat in truck, best view, and best dressed. King of the kids, was Adrian, handsome and spoilt by everyone. After all, he was Ben Fiddler's son, the boss's son, and any friend of Adrian's was a friend of the boss's. And Adrian, if he was nothing else, was lovable, impulsive and reckless.

'Hey!' yelled Paul, beating against the side of the truck. 'Did you know that Miss Godwin was going to the caves?'

'Of course I did,' said Adrian. 'What's wrong with that?'

'You're sending her off on a wild-goose chase. You know as well as I do there aren't any drawings. All she'll get out of it is a broken leg or a broken neck. You've got to tell her.'

Adrian's handsome young face had reddened. 'Are you calling me a liar, Paul Mace?'

'If the cap fits, wear it!'

'You can't talk to me like that. I'm not a liar.'

'I say you are.'

'And I say I'm not.'

Adrian couldn't find the right words. Suddenly, he lost his temper because he was guilty and frightened and had to cover up. He leapt over the side of the truck, his cheeks flaming and his conscience smarting, sure that already he had been disgraced in front of everyone. There truly weren't any drawings and he wondered just how many people knew it. He went over the truck side on top of Paul and bore him down into the dust, shocked, even then, by the silly impulse that had made him do it, terrified while he punched and shouted.

The place was an uproar of women's and children's shrieks and outraged bellows from two or three men. Paul and Adrian were dragged apart and jerked to their feet.

They were filthy and Paul was as frightened as Adrian, because he had fought the boss's son, and there was the boss, now, hanging on to his son, glaring at Paul.

'Well,' demanded Ben Fiddler, 'what's the reason for this disgraceful display?'

'He called me a liar,' hissed Adrian. 'No one calls me a liar, dad. And with everyone listening, too.'

'Did you?' Big Ben glared into Paul's eyes. 'Did you call my son a liar?'

It wasn't fair. That was how it seemed to Paul, because no matter where he looked no one seemed to be friendly, not even his own father and mother. They didn't look friendly. They looked embarrassed.

'Yes, sir,' he stammered.

'And is he a liar?'

What could a thirteen-year-old boy say to that? Because Adrian was his friend. Adrian, for all his faults, was good fun and a good friend. But it was true that there was more at stake than honour. There was Miss Godwin and those dangerous caves; the water that sometimes rushed out of them and the loose rocks and the tricky climb to reach them. He didn't want to hurt Adrian, but he didn't want Miss Godwin to kill herself, because a woman could never climb paths that were not easy for nimble-footed boys.

'He said something, sir,' murmured Paul, 'that wasn't true. I'm sorry, sir, but he told Miss Godwin that there were old aboriginal drawings in the caves and Miss Godwin's going to look for them and she'll be hurt.'

'I know all about the drawings,' barked Ben Fiddler. 'So does everyone, and there's no reason why they shouldn't be there. If Adrian says they're there, that's where they are. You will apologize to my son.'

Somehow the right words seemed to be there and Paul said them like a man. 'I will apologize, sir, if Adrian will come with me and lead Miss Godwin to them. If we don't lead her she'll be hurt.'

Now Ben was a good man and a fair man. He was stern, he was master, but he had his affection for Paul because Paul had grown up with his own son and Paul's parents had come to Hills End at the very beginning, ten years ago. Ben liked Paul and somehow, at this moment, had never liked him more. This lad was in earnest, and he did know that Adrian could be a little devil, and if Paul was prepared to give up his picnic to prove his point Adrian could do the same.

'Very well,' said Ben, 'it's not much use my preaching to you on Sunday mornings if I can't do the right thing on Saturday mornings. Adrian, you will do as Paul says. You will go together with Miss Godwin and take her to the drawings. Then Paul can publicly apologize – or you can!'

Adrian was flabbergasted. 'But it's Picnic Day. This is our Picnic Day.'

'So it is. But if the pair of you choose to settle your arguments like savages – just look at yourselves, you couldn't possibly come as you are – if you act like savages you can do without the pleasures of civilization. And, far from your presence being necessary to protect Miss Godwin, I'll be happy to leave you both in her safe-keeping.' Big Ben turned to Paul's father. 'All right by you?'

Paul's father nodded. There wasn't much else that he could do.

'Settled!' Big Ben clapped his hands together and boomed, 'Everyone aboard! Let's get 'em rolling.' He turned back then to his own son. 'Adrian,' he said, 'I'll be disappointed if those drawings are not there. I want to see your name cleared. Off with you, the pair of you. If you don't get up to the school-house Miss Godwin will be gone without you.'

Adrian didn't know what to say. He had trapped himself in his own lie. There was no way out except to follow the path his father had laid down for him. He'd have to go through with it in the hope that something would turn up to straighten things out. And to miss the picnic – that was punish-ment. That was cruel. His father had been cruel. Paul had been cruel. Life at that moment held no joy for Adrian. If he had been alone he would have cried.

But he wasn't alone. Gussie, that dreadful sister of Paul's, suddenly fastened on her brother's arm. Paul was taken aback; but he shouldn't have been. Perhaps they squabbled like cat and dog, but there wasn't a soul living more loyal than Gussie. She hated her brother and loved him to distraction. She called him every word she could think of but she worshipped him. If Paul were condemned to die Gussie would die with him. She clung to his arm and tears were rolling down her cheeks as she said that if Paul couldn't go to the picnic she wouldn't go either, and that started it.

That started it. It certainly did.

CHAPTER TWO

Miss Elaine Godwin

THAT she was the source of this argument, Miss Elaine Godwin was unaware. She had entered the schoolhouse, and with the door shut and the windows closed, nothing could penetrate but the deep-seated rhythm of the big diesel engine down at the mill.

There were two of those engines installed side by side so that one could be rested and maintained while continuous electrical power was supplied. The beat of one engine or the other was always there, but rarely heard. It was so much a part of the township that few ever noticed it, not even the observant Miss Godwin as she sat now, for a few moments, in the chair she had occupied for nine years.

The classroom was empty of children, yet they were there in the memories that were her only wealth. Children had come and gone; some had stayed at Hills End, but most had gone out into the world and many had never returned. Some

22

had become labourers, some tradesmen, a handful had entered the professions. A few kept in touch with her, but most had vanished into the distant towns or the still more remote cities. In their minds she was an occasional memory, a quaint little spinster quietly dressed, thin but not frail, with her seemingly nondescript hair woven into a tight bun. They never realized how beautiful her hair was, but sometimes they glimpsed a picture of her face, fine, thin, of great kindness but of resolute will. She was not a softie. She had more character than most of her pupils would ever have, but she remembered them with the affection and the humour that one would expect of her. She had had her favourites, the boys and the girls she had loved like a mother, but no one had known, least of all the children themselves.

That was one of the reasons why she didn't go to the picnic – never, not from the first year until now – because it was a family affair. She was frightened of it, because she did not have a family between Friday afternoons and Monday mornings. She'd be alone, an intruder, and the last thing she wanted from anyone was pity. She could endure being alone by herself, but she was terrified of being alone in the midst of people.

Adrian had given her a convincing story of the paintings in the caves and she had not the slightest doubt that they were there. It had been one of her great disappointments that she had not found traces of early aboriginal life in this wild region. The area was right for it. There should have been more traces. Perhaps these caves would lead her towards still more exciting discoveries and provide the climax for her book. She had taught the children for years what to look for and where to look, realizing that wandering boys had more chance of stumbling upon these things than she ever had. In only one way was her excitement tempered. She knew the caves could be dangerous. And she knew that she had turned back from them, years ago, when plain common sense had convinced her that she might fall to her death from the cliff-face. The memory of her fear was still in her mind, but perhaps made more dangerous by the years in which she had thought about it. Nobody had ever been hurt getting into them or out of them. Surely where a boy could go, she could go.

She walked between the desks to the window at the end of the room, her favourite window that looked up the valley, into the cleft of the mountains. There they stood as always, dusky green and purple against the clear sky, but this morning they were a challenge to her. Out there, somewhere, at the foot of a great bluff in the south-west, was the unseen ledge that zigzagged up towards the caves. She realized then, for the first time, that she was trembling, that she was weak, that she truly was afraid.

The schoolroom was hot and suddenly she felt the need of air. She opened the window, but outside there wasn't a breath. The gentle breeze of the early morning had stilled and through the window came the sounds of truck engines starting, of doors slamming.

In a few seconds she would be alone. Frank Tobias might be on duty in the mill, but his world was down there and her world was as far removed from it. She took the book she wanted from the library shelf, collected her things again, her stick, her haversack and her camera, and said a little prayer, 'Watch over them as they go, and watch over me as I go.'

They stood outside the hall and watched the trucks and the cars pull away, raising the dust, until the waving hands were gone round the bend, lost in the dust, and the sound of the engines was a diminishing roar. Already the convoy, the straggle of vehicles, was on the winding road beside the River Magnus, moving deeper into the mountains.

Frank Tobias, the foreman, rocked slowly on his heels, groping for something to say. He couldn't think of anything. He couldn't understand these children and he was pretty sure they couldn't understand themselves either. He was silent and they were silent, stunned perhaps, that their parents had actually gone and that they were actually left behind. Perhaps the clamour that Gussie had led would never have started if the children had really believed that their parents would have allowed them to stay. Perhaps it was that their bluff had been called. Gussie had been in earnest and perhaps Frances had been in earnest, but the others had merely hoped that their voices raised together would have convinced Mr Fiddler that Adrian and Paul should not be left behind. It hadn't worked that way. They were all left behind, all seven of them – Adrian, Paul, Gussie, Frances, Butch, Harvey, and Maisie. The trucks were gone and would not be back until midnight or even later. They had missed the picnic. It was awful. They couldn't believe it.

Frank Tobias slowly filled his pipe. As a rule he never smoked before ten in the morning, but in his own way he was so upset by the whole business that he had to do something with his hands, and his pipe came most readily to them. So he filled his pipe and watched the thunderstruck children and had to blink back his own tears when Gussie started crying again and little Harvey Collins began to sniffle. He blamed Ben Fiddler. The right word at the right time and it wouldn't have happened. Ben was such a stickler for what he considered to be the fair and proper thing; but this was neither fair nor proper. It was just a darned shame.

'Kids,' he said, at last, 'you've made your own beds, you know. You'll have to lie in them. I'm sorry, kids, but you'll have to make the best of it. Go home and fix yourselves some lunch. I'll chase after Miss Godwin, and tell her to wait. All right?'

Paul turned a hostile eye on Adrian. 'It's all your fault,' he said. 'You and your big whoppers!'

'Enough of that,' snapped the foreman. 'You kids are not going to solve your problem by dwelling on it. You're all as much to blame as the other. Perhaps you'll learn a lesson from it – not to tempt your elders too far. You didn't think they'd do it to you and I didn't either, but I'm not a father. Go on home. Get your lunches.'

Miss Godwin was stopped by a voice calling her name. She was sure, for a moment or two, that she must have imagined it, for when she looked back she could see no one. She could see nothing of life except the smoke from a few kitchen fires, not yet burnt out, rising vertically, and the still persistent dust haze lying over the road and the rooftops.

'Miss Godwin!'

There was no doubt that time. She was certainly being called and it could have been by none other than Frank Tobias.

'Yes, Mr Tobias. This way.'

She saw him then, trudging up the steep path from the road, obviously breathless, and wiping sweat from his forehead with the back of his hand. A pleasant man, this one. Kept to himself. Minded his own business. But always near at hand when something needed to be done. A widower was Mr Tobias; his wife had died seven years ago.

He came up to her. 'Must be getting old,' he panted.

'Aren't we all? What's the trouble, Mr Tobias?'

'Much too much trouble for my liking.'

'Indeed?'

'Seven of the children have been left behind. There was a fight between young Adrian and Paul.'

'Left behind, Mr Tobias, because two boys had a fight?' Miss Godwin was astonished. 'Boys will always fight, Mr Tobias. If a boy doesn't have a fight occasionally there's something wrong with the boy. What's wrong with our older generation? Have they forgotten they were young themselves. Left them behind? Oh dear, dear, dear!'

Frank Tobias never quite knew how to handle this unusual woman, but he did his best. 'There's more to it than that, Miss Godwin. The children asked me specially not to tell you why, but I think you'd better know. It concerns you.'

Miss Godwin's heart began to flutter. She couldn't even guess how it concerned her, but she was afraid it might have been sentimental nonsense, or even worse, pity for her, because she was alone. Suddenly, she went very pale. She was more full of pity for her fellow men and women than anyone within miles of her, but she could not bear to become the object of pity herself.

She leant on her walking-stick and forced herself to speak calmly. 'Very well, Mr Tobias. Perhaps you'd better tell me.'

He told her the story from the beginning to that sullen end he had witnessed, seven unhappy children making their ways to their respective homes. Perhaps it wasn't as bad as she had feared. She was saddened, but touched that Paul should have been concerned for her safety. That was the root of it – her safety and the possibility that Adrian had lied. Of course, Adrian hadn't lied. Really, she was rather annoyed with Paul. He had shown much less than his usual good sense. He had jumped to conclusions, something she had endeavoured to teach her children never to do. It didn't occur to her that she was jumping to conclusions herself.

'Very well,' she said. 'As far as I am concerned you have not told me. What the children elect to say is their own business. I will wait for them here ... Good morning, Mr Tobias.'

The foreman didn't know what to do with himself. He had been given his marching orders. No question about it. He made a nervous grimace – a mannerism of his when he was embarrassed – tapped out his still unlit pipe on his heel, and wandered back down the hill, feeling uncommonly like a little boy rebuffed for telling tales out of turn. School-teachers! He snorted. They were a funny race of people!

Miss Elaine Godwin sat on a stump and took from her haversack the book she had removed from the library shelf. It was called *The Art of the Aboriginal*.

She knew it from cover to cover and probably that was why she couldn't concentrate. She couldn't get out of her mind a suspicion that Frank Tobias had made up the whole story. Perhaps it was pity all the time. Perhaps the children, perhaps all the people, were sorry for her. That would be perfectly dreadful. It worried her so much that she started trembling again, all over.

CHAPTER THREE

The Ascent Begins

ADRIAN was first back to the hall. He wasn't going to let anyone think that he was frightened to face it, so he was back before the quickest of them. There was only one escape for him. He'd have to bluff it through. There were so many caves, anyway, that he could pretend to lose his bearings. Who could know that he hadn't really lost his bearings? There were hundreds of caves. The more he thought about it, the better he began to feel.

Frances came down the road, thinking ruefully of the truck convoy drawing nearer and nearer to the big bridge at Fiddler's Crossing, thinking of all the shops in Stanley, full of such wonderful things, pretty dresses and long lengths of beautiful material, things she wouldn't have bought, but things she would have looked at, up and down the long main street, all through the hot afternoon, window-shopping with her mother, dreaming.

'Hi,' said Adrian.

'Hi,' said Frances.

Harvey came down the track, small, squeaky, pugnacious little Harvey, nine years old, as sharp as a tack, full of fight and courage, the terror of every girl who wore pigtails or hair at all, a very dangerous young fellow when roused. He fought like a wasp, darting in and out. He lived for a rough and tumble. More often than not his poor father was black and blue.

'Hi,' said Adrian.

'Hi yourself,' said Harvey.

Maisie came along, wondering how on earth she had come to be mixed up in it, because no one was more harmless than Maisie. She was clever at school, well behaved at home, and only eleven years old. Quiet as she usually was, Maisie had a twinkle in her eye, and perhaps that was why she had jumped from the truck, following the leader, eager for the prank. But it wasn't so marvellous now. No, it wasn't so marvellous now.

'Hi,' said Adrian.

'Hullo,' said Maisie.

Butch – his mother called him Christopher – waddled into view with an enormous lunch bulging from his school-bag. He hadn't emptied the refrigerator because there was always tomorrow, but he had made a big hole in it. Butch needed food and a lot of it because Butch was almost as big as a man. He had tumbled from the truck because Adrian was in trouble and Adrian was a frequent provider of malted milks and chocolate bars. But Butch liked Adrian, too, apart from that, because most of the time Adrian was a very nice fellow.

'Hi,' said Adrian.

'Hi.' Butch smiled.

Paul and Gussie came along the road, guiltily, sure they had ruined the day for everyone. Gussie felt it very badly, because Gussie was all gold. She was the light in her parents' eyes; she was everybody's darling, nearly twelve, with not a shred of conceit in her. Everybody's darling, that is, except Paul's. As far as he was concerned, she was Trouble with a capital T.

'Hi, you two,' said Adrian.

Paul looked him up and down and again began to wonder whether he should blame himself entirely. Adrian's lie was the real cause. Adrian was at the bottom of it, the big show-off.

'It's hot,' said Paul, 'isn't it?'

Adrian shrugged. 'Cold's the word, more like it. Talk about the cold shoulder!'

'Well, you've asked for it,' Paul said angrily.

'Please,' appealed Frances. 'We've all been silly. Don't let's make it worse. Mr Tobias told us to make the best of it and I think that was good advice. Why spoil Miss Godwin's day along with everyone else's?'

'That's right,' agreed Butch.

'Where is Mr Tobias, anyway?' asked Paul. 'He mightn't have even found Miss Godwin.'

'I saw him go down to the mill five minutes ago.' Adrian took his first pace up the road. 'Let's get started, eh? I want to get to those caves and listen to your apology?'

Gussie flared in her loyalty to Paul. 'You're the one that'll be apologizing, Adrian Fiddler. You're just a big fibber.'

'Them's fightin' words,' squealed Harvey, shaping up. 'Who wants a fight?'

'Please, please,' said Frances.

'Yes, pipe down, Junior,' growled Paul. 'You, too, Gussie. We don't want Miss Godwin to know we've been scrapping.'

'That's right,' said Butch.

They started up the road towards the schoolhouse, not very friendly one towards the other, in a straggling line.

'What *are* we going to tell Miss Godwin, anyway?' said Maisie mildly. Maisie was like that. She often came out with

31

the awkward question, probably because she took more time off to think.

Adrian faltered in his stride, and stopped. 'Yeah,' he said. 'What?'

'Golly, I don't know,' said Paul. 'We – we can't tell her the truth. She'd feel awful.'

'Any more awful than we feel?' suggested Frances.

'That's different,' said Paul. 'She's bound to find out sooner or later, but not now. She'll find out when we get up there and can't find the drawings. I reckon that'll be soon enough.'

'But there are drawings.' Adrian was getting angry again. 'I told you I wasn't a liar. The drawings *are* there. You're not fighting fairly. You won't even believe me. You won't even give me a chance.'

'I believe you,' said Frances, 'and Paul isn't fair. He's being very unkind.' It hurt Frances to say that, but she had to be honest. 'If you don't give Adrian a chance to prove himself, Paul, you'll be even more in the wrong.'

'I'm not in the wrong now. I could punch him in the jaw, the great big show-off.'

Harvey started shaping up again, grinning all over his face, and Butch backed away, a couple of quiet paces down the hill, but Maisie saved the day. Maisie had asked the question and she answered it. While everyone else had been arguing, she had worked it out.

'I think,' said Maisie, 'you'd better tell her, Adrian, that we'd planned it as a surprise for her, but it wasn't until this morning that we could persuade our parents to let us go with her. It's not a real fib, you know, is it?'

'That's right,' said Butch.

Perhaps it wasn't a real fib at that.

Miss Godwin heard them coming and continued to read her

book, or continued to make out that she was reading it. She was very nervous. For the first time in her life she was frightened of a few children – not of what they could do to her, but of what they had probably done already. She didn't even try to believe Mr Tobias's story any longer. Perhaps a little of it might have been true, but she was sure its whole meaning had been changed. Perhaps the whole thing had been staged. Perhaps these children had been forced by their parents to go with her when their poor little hearts must have longed to go on the picnic. Parents had done crueller things out of a misguided sense of duty.

'Hullo, Miss Godwin.'

She trembled and closed her book and noted each from the youngest to the eldest, observed that some had been crying, some were pale, and that all were trying to smile. She fell into the old familiar pattern of schoolroom procedure. 'Good morning, children. It's a lovely day. The sun is shining. We'll take our first lesson out of doors.'

She knew she was talking nonsense, but saved herself with a slow smile, and they thought she was making a joke.

'Miss Godwin,' said Adrian awkwardly, 'I – I suppose you're wondering why we're here?'

'Adrian, I have long since ceased to wonder about children. But I see you have your lunches with you.'

'Yes, miss. We want to know if we can come with you?'

'You may.'

'"Cos – well – we planned it as a surprise.'

'You've surprised me all right. Yes, you have. A very pleasant surprise. Shall we start then? We have a long way to go.'

Adrian was floundering a little. 'You – you don't want to hear any more?'

'No.' Miss Godwin stepped from her stump, brushed a few ants from her jodhpurs, and smiled again. 'I told you, I have long since ceased to wonder about children. Come along.'

Again she heaved up her haversack, squared her thin shoulders, and they had no choice but to follow with pounding hearts and not a little confusion. Frances was the only one mature enough to observe that everything was not right with Miss Godwin. Frances was no older than Paul or Adrian or Butch in years, but much older in wisdom. She knew that something was wrong, but that was as far as her reasoning went. Admittedly the others thought it was odd, but all grown-ups were peculiar anyway. Grown-ups were like the wind. One hour they blew in one direction, the next hour in another. At least with kids a fellow knew where he was. A bully on Monday was a bully on Tuesday, but one never knew what grown-ups were going to say or do next. Very peculiar.

So they set off through the ever-rising succession of lesser hills and gullies that lay between them and the great bluff, wading through the many streams, or jumping them, or crossing them over fallen logs or rocks. No distant throb reached them from the trucks so long gone, no voices apart from their own, no sound except the cracking of twigs, the hissing and whispering and rushing of water, the mysterious groaning of big trees, and the birds and the distant dogs. The dogs were back home in Hills End and were very annoyed about it. Almost every dog in the town was attached to a stake in the ground, a running wire, or a kennel. They wailed into the morning air until they realized that no one was coming to release them and one by one accepted that it was better to doze in the sun or gnaw a bone.

All sound except the beating of the diesel eased away through the hills like the dying of a pain. The fires went out, the smoke vanished, the sun blazed down, the dust was still, and Frank Tobias in the office at the mill nodded over his book until his head dropped and his eyes closed.

Everything went to sleep except the great River Magnus. It

writhed and rippled and rumbled and cried out its warning, but no one heard.

'I think,' said Miss Elaine Godwin at precisely ten o'clock, 'that we will take time off for recess.'

It was a good idea, and Butch, in particular, agreed wholeheartedly.

Miss Godwin added, 'Ten minutes, children. One mustn't rest for too long or one will lose the urge to keep going.'

They flopped down on the last ridge short of the bluff and here the ground was too rocky even for stunted trees to grow. It was barren, except for tenacious little wild flowers, a few grasses and a few isolated bushes. It was frightfully hot and they sheltered in the shade of boulders.

Miss Godwin took an apple from her haversack and began to eat it, thoughtfully and slowly, chewing each mouthful twenty-two times, sitting erect, shoulders squared, eyes puckered against the glare. She was very, very tired. She had forgotten that she was getting older, that the last time she had come here she had not been compelled to set an example to a group of children, that she had not been distressed for any reason at all, and that she had not been afraid until she had actually reached the bluff.

Paul peeled an orange and he could feel his heart thudding against his ribs and he ached all through. Miss Godwin had set too fast a pace. She was tough. My word, she was tough! Boys liked to stop and start, to poke under logs, to drink from springs, to throw stones into pools. Boys liked to take their time and if they didn't get to their destination no harm was done.

Poor Butch was nearly finished. His feet were sore, he was soaked in sweat, he wanted to lie down and sleep. He was too weary even to eat.

Gussie panted in the shade, longing for a tall glass of home-made ginger beer. She felt she wanted to cry. She couldn't understand why Miss Godwin had to hurry, hurry, hurry. Usually her nature walks were fun. This was awful.

Frances was hot and bothered and worn out. She knew now that something really was wrong with Miss Godwin. She wasn't her usual self at all. She seemed to have retired into another room. Her face had never looked so thin and tight.

But Adrian stared at the bluff, half a mile away across this rocky gap, rearing up and up, hazed over with heat, not frying in the sun, but toasting in the sun, browner and browner. A rugged face of rock so huge it looked like the wall at the end of the world, and this gap in front of him was the moat at the end of the world. There was water in the moat as there had been since time began, always running, trickling, rushing, welling up from the depths of the earth or oozing from the wall or cascading from some immense height above it. Here they had come to find the drawings that weren't there.

Paul, Adrian was sure, didn't understand him. They were so close but so far apart. Paul was too precise, too accurate in everything he said or did. All Paul was interested in was the truth. Adrian liked to look for things beyond the truth; he liked to romance; he liked to create things, not out of logs of wood or lumps of stone, but out of his mind, with a pencil in his hand or a brush, or nothing at all in his hand. He only had to close his eyes and he could see things that weren't there. The drawings weren't really a lie. Adrian had created them for himself. They only became a lie when other people believed they were real. And they had believed him. And then he had lied to protect himself.

'Very well, children. Time's up.'

'Please, miss.' Butch turned his eyes on her, great big pleading eyes. 'Please, miss,' he said, 'but d'you think I could stay here? Honest, miss, me feet are killin' me.'

Miss Godwin clucked, '"*My feet*", Christopher, "are *killing* me".'

'Are they, miss? Oh, I'm sorry, miss.'

'Not my feet, Christopher. Your feet.'

Butch blinked. 'That's right, miss. They're killin' me. Honest.'

Miss Godwin clucked again. 'I cannot leave you here, Christopher. That would never do. Oh dear, no. The sun is far, far too hot.'

'Gee, miss!'

'If your feet are hurting you so much it would be wiser if you hobbled another hundred yards or so until we found a nice pool in the shade where you could soak them. Does that sound better?'

'Yes, miss. Thank you, miss.'

'Come along, children.'

They trailed after her, down through the boulders and the gravel, past the dead wood and the debris dumped there by the violence of forgotten storms, and Butch hobbled and grunted and winced and sweated. His heels were blistered because his shoes were tight. They had been shining new shoes, size ten, specially for the picnic. What a picnic! There would have been ice-creams and lemon drinks and big, juicy pies.

'Here you are, Christopher, a nice pool and a nice rock for shade. Now you soak your feet and get them right again and then come along after us. Do you know where the caves are?'

'Yes, miss.'

'Very well. When you get to the path at the bottom call loudly for us and we'll let you know exactly where we are.'

'Yes, miss.'

'Don't drop your new shoes in the water, will you?'

'No, miss.'

'Come along, children.'

Again they trailed after her, looking back at Butch, pulling faces at him, and little Harvey mocked him by limping like a man with a wooden leg.

They disappeared amongst the rocks and Butch eased off his new shoes that weren't shiny any more, and were scuffed on the toes, and so terribly tight at the heels. The blisters had burst and it hurt him to peel his socks off, but then he shivered in delight when he lowered his feet into the cool, kind water. In a minute or two he felt much better, much cooler all over, and he unbuckled his school-bag and ate a large piece of apple pie.

When he tried to put his shoes on again he couldn't. His feet started hurting almost as much as before, so there was only one thing he could do. He curled up in the shade of the over-hanging rock and went to sleep.

At the foot of the bluff Miss Godwin gathered her children round her. She was guilty of deceiving them. They thought she only wanted to talk but really she wanted to rest. She felt like a jelly inside, quivery and without any strength. She knew now that this climb up the bluff was every bit as bad as she had feared. This was why she hadn't climbed it when she had come before; it had been simply common sense, not cowardice.

She drew her book from her haversack and it fell open at a photograph of the rock paintings at Lightning Totem Centre in North Australia.

'... Now take a good look at these, Adrian, and tell me if you find any similarities to what you saw.'

Adrian had been through this before. 'No,' he said.

'You're sure?'

'Certain, miss.'

'I'm going to ask you once more, Adrian, to go through the book from cover to cover and make your selection. There must be similarities somewhere.'

'I told you about the red hands, miss.'

'That doesn't help much, Adrian. There are thousands of red hands throughout the continent. It is their association with these other things that is mystifying.'

Paul sighed inwardly. Of course the association was mystifying. It wasn't even true. But Miss Godwin had spoken about this, over and over again. She was excited by it. She had kept harping on it, perhaps trying to break Adrian's story down, but Adrian's story had never broken. He hadn't changed a detail. He had described things which, Miss Godwin said, had never been found before. They must have been made a very long time ago, perhaps thousands of years ago, by artists out of touch with all other men.

So she waited while Adrian thumbed over the book again, from photograph to photograph, endeavouring to steady her nerves and marshal her strength. How she wished these children hadn't come! Their very presence forced her to make the climb. She couldn't get out of it with dignity. If she failed to make the climb what would these children think of a teacher who taught them to explore but was afraid to explore herself? What would they think of a teacher who enthused about the art of the stone-age men but was too frightened to make a personal effort to see it?

'Really, miss,' said Adrian, closing the book and passing it back to her, 'it might be that I've forgotten, but I'm sure they were different.'

'Very well, Adrian.' Miss Godwin glanced at her watch. 'We'll find out how good an explorer you are. I think you'd better lead the way with Paul, don't you, and the rest of us can follow very carefully?'

'Yes, miss. There's no danger really. It looks much worse than it is. There's only one thing. Don't look down unless you've got something to hang on to.'

'Do you hear that, children? Adrian says there's no danger

and Adrian knows. But if any of you would rather stay down here just say the word.'

Gussie would have liked to have stayed, very, very much, but she was frightened that everyone would tease her. She didn't like the look of the water trickling from the rocks, or the moss and the slime. And her legs were aching, with the awful ache that she got sometimes and that her mother called 'growing pains'. It didn't seem right that it hurt to grow, Gussie thought, but perhaps that was why the trees groaned sometimes. Perhaps it hurt them, too.

Maisie, too, was rather anxious, but she was frightened to speak up, frightened that everyone would make fun of her.

'If it is an important discovery,' she said, 'will we all be famous?'

'I don't know about that,' said Miss Godwin. 'Adrian will be the famous one. We'll have to name the discovery after him.'

'Golly!' said Paul, shaken for the moment. 'Can we do that?'

'Of course we can. It's our right, and if the Government agrees the caves will be known by his name for ever and ever.'

'No kiddin'?' queried Adrian.

Miss Godwin coughed discreetly. 'That isn't quite the word, Adrian, but it is a fact. They'll be named in your honour.' Perhaps she was rueful then. She wasn't selfish, but it would have been nice if they had suggested the discovery be named after her. She couldn't expect children to think of that.

'I'll tell you what,' she said, 'because we've all come here today, I'll write a special chapter in my book and put down all your names, and then all of us can bask in Adrian's glory. Do you like that for an idea?'

They certainly liked that and all talked at once and Gussie even forgot her growing pains.

'Come along then. Let's start.'

CHAPTER FOUR

Danger

FRANK TOBIAS, the foreman, woke up with a headache and a stiff neck. He blinked in the direction of the big clock on the office wall and was vaguely surprised. It was five minutes past eleven.

He had a stale taste in his mouth and his nostrils seemed to be blocked and that dull ache in his head throbbed and throbbed. He shouldn't have allowed himself to fall asleep. Nothing sapped more life from a man than sleeping in broad daylight with the sun blazing against the window panes and down upon a creaking iron roof.

He had brought a vacuum flask from his home and he poured a mug of tea and panted while he sipped it, because it was difficult to breathe. He felt as though he had had his head in a bag, felt half suffocated, and even a little squeamish. Then he realized that something was wrong, something was missing.

41

The silence, apart from the occasional creaking in the roof, was complete.

Suddenly, he lurched from his chair. The engine had stopped. Great Scott! What had happened to the diesel? And then he knew. He hadn't refuelled it. It was always refuelled at eight. That upset over the kids had put it out of his mind. What a fine thing! The foreman of all people! If Ben Fiddler couldn't trust his foreman whom could he trust? That meant every refrigerator in town would be defrosting, even the big freezing chamber in the shop for the meat, and the butter melting, and the milk turning sour. Glory, what a mess there'd be, with an outside temperature already in the nineties!

And there was another thing. If the diesel really was out of fuel, there'd be a job to do, and what a beastly job! The pipe lines all full of air, sludge from the empty tank sucked into the cylinders of the engine. It'd take hours to get the brute started again. Only one thing to do. Get number two engine turning over and roll up his sleeves and strip down number one. Glory, old Ben would skin him alive!

He hurried from the office, across the heat of the sizzling yard, that yard that was inches deep in wood shavings, towards the engine house. What a place it would be on a day like this – galvanized iron walls, galvanized iron roof – a man would cook in his own juice!

He stopped then, suddenly disturbed. It was the feel of the yard, the feel of the heat, the stillness, the deathly calm, the suffocating atmosphere. He'd never felt anything quite like it. Sweat began pouring from him. Perhaps it was more than sleep that had made him squeamish.

Instinctively he looked up to the sky. Unclouded, but not clear. Great Scott! In the north-east it looked ghastly, glazed over with a bronze sheen.

He stared at it, couldn't understand it, had never seen anything like it; but he knew it was wrong.

He felt helpless, alone, isolated.

A man was equal to things made by men, but Nature was different. There were times when Nature could be tamed, but there were times when Nature couldn't be stopped.

He realized he was listening again, and the stillness that he had taken to be total silence was neither stillness nor silence. He could hear dogs crying and the River Magnus rumbling, and he could see a cat across the yard in the hot shade, standing erect, bristling. A flight of ducks winged across the valley at an hour that was unusual for them, heading south. He could hear the lowing of cattle – the bull and the five cows and the calves at Rickard's place. The milking of the cows for the coming evening was his responsibility. He could feel and hear and sense many things and all became one emotion – alarm.

It demanded a conscious effort to continue to the engine house. No matter what was heralded by the state of the sky, one engine or the other had to be started immediately before all the perishable food in the township was ruined. He was right about the fuel. Number one was sucked dry. Frank Tobias was disgusted with himself, because when he felt the engine he knew it had been idle for an hour at least. The exhaust pipe was comparatively cool. He started the emergency unit and got back into the yard.

He was restless and wondered how far the picnic convoy had gone. Probably most of the way. By now they'd be no more than thirty minutes' journey from Stanley, all going well, with no punctures or breakdowns.

He wondered about Miss Godwin and the children. They certainly would have reached their destination. Provided there had been no loitering they could have walked to the bluff in a little over two hours. There'd be no loitering with Miss Godwin. She bustled everywhere she went, as though her next hour were her last.

He mopped his brow and wondered about himself. He was

a strong man and a good man, but even the strong and the good might feel uneasy at being alone, as he was now, in an empty township, with a mighty barrier of mountains standing between him and the next man. The woman and the kids didn't count. If anything went wrong they'd be dependent on him. They'd be looking to him for help. He couldn't turn to them.

And something *was* wrong. He knew that more certainly than he had ever known anything. If he had been trapped at the rim of an erupting volcano he couldn't have been more alarmed. The feel of the sky, the feel of the heat, the feel of the air, were downright evil.

He stirred himself and paced down to the river. Old man Magnus was the weather prophet. Old man Magnus was the crystal ball that told the future.

He stood at the bank and shivered. The water was dark, running high, rumbling. Glory, the river was almost yelling at him!

He stumbled back to the mill across the flats.

The heat indeed was very trying and Miss Elaine Godwin shuffled up the face of the bluff, perspiring freely, shaking so much at the knees that she was sure they were knocking together. Dear, dear, dear! Why couldn't she act her age and admit it was too much for her? She was groaning for breath and her pulse was beating so hard in her temples that all she could hear was its thud-thud-thud.

She was such a fool. Here she was, condoning this danger, encouraging these children to risk their lives, when she should have forbidden this exercise. Exercise? Indeed no. It was a criminally foolish escapade which might leave her responsible for injury or death. Those dreadful parents sending their children after her! It was too much responsibility altogether. And, bless her soul, she'd have to get down again afterwards. That would be worse by far. It was this continual patter of little stones, and the times she slipped on wet rocks or slime, the times she looked down because the depths drew her eyes with a dreadful fascination, the times she groped for a foothold and sent a shower of fragments on the children beneath her. The times she was giddy and her head swam, the times she wanted to scream at the top of her voice, yet had to say so calmly, 'Come along, children.'

Suddenly she was there, on the wide ledge that formed the opening to a cave, and Paul was smiling at her and Adrian seemed unusually subdued.

'Well, well, well,' she said breathlessly. 'Here we are.'

Harvey, Gussie, Maisie, and finally Frances came up on the ledge behind her. The girls were flushed and excited, full of their achievement because not too many girls had got as far as this before. They had been surprised to discover that the way up was far less dangerous than they had been told. Of course, they had had to be careful, but no more careful than in climbing a tree.

Miss Godwin was still fluttery and was finding it difficult to conceal her distress. All she wanted to do was sit down, and she never knew how she resisted the yearning. She was a brave soul and a far better leader than she gave herself credit for. They never dreamt that she was frightened, never imagined the state of her mind.

'Now, Adrian,' she said, 'we're in your hands.'

'Have you brought a torch, Miss Godwin?'

'Of course. Of course. Always prepared.'

Adrian wished most fervently that she hadn't been. That had been a possible way out for him – no torch – and even now perhaps if the torch were small enough he might contrive to flatten the battery; but no, Miss Godwin's torch was an electric lantern, six volts, and its power would last for days.

'Is it very far in, Adrian?'

'No, miss. So long as we find the right cave it's only a few yards.'

'Goodness!' Miss Godwin was rather stern. 'You have no doubt that you can find it?'

'Oh, no. It might take a little time, but I'll find it.'

'Very well. As I said, we're in your hands. Take the torch. We don't know how soon we'll need it. The sunlight won't last for ever.'

It was Gussie who was left behind. She was so enthralled by the great rock bed lying beneath her that these silly caves pitting the face of the bluff seemed unimportant. She had climbed high, right up here, and the view was the reward, the depth of space, the impression that she was sitting in an aeroplane looking over the side. She was sure she could see the pool where Butch had stopped, sure she could see him lying in the shade. She simply didn't notice the sky until suddenly there were no shadows.

She glanced up and the sun had vanished behind the strangest-looking cloud she had ever seen. It seemed to have reached out of the north like a big black arm and closed its hand round the sun.

'Ooh,' she said. 'Look at that.'

She turned, and there was no one to look. They'd all gone.

'Oh, bother!' she said. 'Wait for me. *Wait for me!*'

At a minute to twelve Frank Tobias switched on the wireless for the midday news. He was certain that if this great mass of ugly cloud meant anything at all there would be reports of its progress in other regions. Wireless reception was always difficult at Hills End and, despite the fact that the people had raised their aerials to considerable heights, it was the exception to listen in comfort. Short-wave transmission from Radio Australia and from countries to the north of the continent were easier to pick up than 'local' broadcasts. The nearest 'local' transmitter was fully two hundred and fifty miles away. When Frank switched the set on he realized he was cut off even from that comfort. Reception was not marked by the usual fading but by an alarming crash of static. He hastily switched it off again.

Already the first gusts of cold air were swirling dust-clouds through Hills End, loose sheets of iron were clanking, windows were rattling, and everywhere dogs were wailing.

The foreman was now very ill at ease. There were too many things about this sky and the atmosphere that he didn't like. He had not been able to subdue his initial alarm. He told himself repeatedly that Hills End had weathered many storms in the past, but no matter how often or how earnestly he called himself a fool his fears welled up again.

He ran from the office up into the main street, and began racing from house to house, shutting every window and door.

Butch woke up with an uneasy, unhappy feeling. He felt cold, even frightened, and didn't know why it should be.

He sat up, realized quickly enough where he was and why, but couldn't understand the gloom. At first he thought he must have slept through to the evening and was hurt that the others had forgotten him, had gone home without him; he was even apprehensive of walking those miles back through the rugged bush, alone, in the dark.

Then something told him that he had not slept very long at all. He just didn't feel as though he had slept for hours, and the peculiar popping sounds that he had been listening to were enormous raindrops hitting the rocks. The sky was black and fierce and in the distance was the unceasing roll of angry thunder. That was why he was uneasy, and he was cold because an icy wind was blustering round him.

Butch scrambled to his feet because he could see that the sky was going to split apart. He knew that when the rain really started it would be a deluge. And as soon as he was on his feet he remembered his blisters and his new shoes and that it was almost half a mile to the bluff where Miss Godwin and the others would be. Butch didn't know which way to run. He had to get his shoes on somehow, because his feet had always been the tender sort, the sort that didn't take too kindly to carrying their owner without a good slab of leather between skin and ground.

He'd never get to the caves. If he went on he would be caught in the open. If he turned back he might have time to scramble into the shelter of the forest. Those huge raindrops were popping more often and he could see jagged lightning flashes striking between earth and cloud.

No. He couldn't go that way, because it was dangerous under the trees when the lightning struck; yet it was terrifying in the open. Each was as bad as the other. Why hadn't he hobbled on with Miss Godwin? Then he'd be cosy and safe inside the caves. Oh, why had he worn his new shoes? If only he'd changed into something old! He couldn't get them on. He couldn't stand the pain. Even his toes seemed to be swollen now.

He started whimpering. He might have been almost as big as a man, but in so many ways he was only a little boy. He tucked his shoes under his arm and first went one way, and then another, and then back to the rock again beside the pool. Soon he was sobbing and he wriggled in hard against the rock on the sheltered side and down came the rain with a horrifying clap of thunder. In seconds he was drenched to the skin.

CHAPTER FIVE

The Storm

'GOODNESS!' exclaimed Miss Elaine Godwin. 'What was that?'

She knew what it was, really, but she was so accustomed to putting questions to children that she felt obliged to ask.

'That was thunder,' said Frances.

'Thunder, indeed. I hope we're all not going to get wet on the way home.'

She wasn't thinking that at all. Her only thought was her fear of descending the bluff. If rain came with the thunder the footholds would be like glass, and somehow she was sure it was raining; although these caves were warm there was in the air the touch and smell of water or ice.

'Children,' she said, 'I think we'd better go back to the entrance to see what's happening.'

'I'll go, miss,' said Paul. 'I know my way. I'll only be half a minute.'

'Thank you all the same, Paul, but we must keep together. We have only the one torch, and I don't wish to be left in the dark, nor do I wish you to be stumbling alone in the dark. Lead the way, Adrian.'

'Fancy a storm on a day like this!' said Gussie. 'Ooh!'

'Yes, Augusta?' said Miss Godwin. 'What did you mean by that tone of surprise?'

'I must have seen it coming. I saw a cloud. The funniest cloud you ever saw.'

Miss Godwin shivered. 'What was funny about it, Augusta?'

'It was like a big black arm, reaching across the sky, taking hold of the sun.'

'You should have told me, child.' Her voice was so sharp that they were surprised. 'Hurry on, Adrian. If there's to be a storm we must get out of here.'

They followed the beam of the torch, this way and that way, but Miss Godwin was bustling so busily on Adrian's heels that she confused him and he took the wrong turning. He wasn't certain in his mind that he was wrong, but the doubt was there, and Paul said, 'Not this way, Adrian.'

'We'll leave that to Adrian, shall we?' snapped Miss Godwin.

'But he might be right, miss,' stammered Adrian. 'I – I think he is right.'

'Nonsense. I distinctly remember this chamber. Hurry on.'

But Adrian knew he didn't remember it, not from any of his journeys in here, and when the pale whiteness of old bones moved into the beam of the torch he was certain he'd never set foot in this cave before.

He heard the sharp intake of Miss Godwin's breath close to his ear, heard the squeal from Harvey and the gasp from Paul.

'Wait!'

Miss Godwin took the torch from Adrian and directed it

across the floor of the cave to a ledge. There were many bones, huge bones, and kangaroo skulls twice as large as any they had ever seen, and on the walls beyond were red hands and black hands and white hands and drawings of animals and devil men.

Miss Godwin sighed, a deep, shuddering sigh, and Gussie cried out, and Paul was so ashamed he wished the ground would open up and swallow him.

Adrian was panting in wonderment, in amazement, in absolute elation. They were here. The drawings *were* here. And they'd called him a liar. That prim and proper Paul had called him a liar and he wasn't a liar at all.

'I'm sorry, Adrian,' Paul murmured. 'Golly, I am sorry!'

Adrian couldn't trust himself to speak, and neither could Miss Godwin. She was too overcome even to consider that Paul's remark confirmed Frank Tobias's story and that all her fears as to the real motives of the children were without foundation.

Frances, strangely, was a little saddened. She had believed Adrian yet she was sorry that Paul had been proved wrong – and Gussie was all confused. She had been so sure that Adrian had been lying. So very, very sure, because Paul had been so sure.

Suddenly all were talking at once, and Miss Godwin had to raise her voice to a shout. 'Be quiet!'

She waited a few moments. 'That's better. That's very much better. Now, no one is to touch a single thing. Before we make any examination I want to photograph everything just as we find it ... Adrian, this is a most wonderful, wonderful discovery. My only regret is that I didn't come a week ago. Imagine it, children – Hills End will be famous. We'll have anthropologists coming here. Great scholars from all over the world. Children, children, this is the most wonderful thing that has ever happened to us. Oh dear, I – I'm really so excited. I'm all of a flutter. Adrian, my boy.' She thrust her arm round him and hugged him tight. 'Why didn't you tell us about the bones, too? Didn't you think they were important? They're the bones of the giant kangaroo – and the diprotodon, I think. Adrian, Adrian, these animals have been extinct for tens of thousands – perhaps hundreds of thousands – of years . . . Goodness me, I'm all of a flutter! I – I cannot believe my eyes. I'm going to wake up in a minute. Oh dear, dear, dear!'

'You won't wake up, Miss Godwin,' said Paul. 'It's real. Really and truly real.'

She sighed again, a shivering and breathless sigh. 'Take the torch, Paul. Shine it on my haversack. I – I must get my things.'

She was trembling so much she could hardly undo the straps and she took out her camera and her tripod and her flashlight fittings, and suddenly heard the thunder-claps again and felt the cold air that was rapidly expelling the warmth from the caves.

She looked up with a troubled frown and slowly stood erect, leaving her precious equipment at her feet. 'First of all,' she said, 'I think we'd better take a look at the weather. We mustn't lose our sense of proportion. These drawings will be here tomorrow – next week – they'll remain. We must take a look at the weather.'

'*Now*, miss?'

'Certainly, Adrian. But we must make sure that we don't lose our cave. It took a long while to find it, even though you were sure you knew where it was. Now, what shall we do?'

'I'll go, miss,' said Paul. 'I said before it would be all right.'

'No. We stay together. While you're with me you're my responsibility.' She paused then and could feel something like a cold hand touching her. There was Christopher – Butch – out there, somewhere in the storm. If it were a storm. It might only be sound and harmless fury. There had been no warning of a storm. This was some trick of the weather. Some local disturbance . . . . 'Now what shall we do? Of course, what we want is a ball of string. That's it. A ball of string. Always be prepared, children. That's the division between the foolish and the wise.'

She took the ball of string from her haversack, tied the loose end round a heavy stone, and directed Paul to proceed in front with the torch while she paid out the string behind her.

So they came again towards the opening, towards a world of frightening sound and vivid lightning flashes, of bitter cold, of violent wind, of torrential rain and hailstones. The hailstones struck the ledge and bounced and were as big as golf-balls. They couldn't approach the opening. They had to stop well back, clear of showering ice and wind-driven rain. The world beyond was like a block of frosted glass – water, ice, and wind in a mass through which they could not see.

That cold feeling that had reached for Miss Godwin crept through her until she was filled with the chill of horror. She clenched her hands tightly and began to pray, saying nothing aloud, but pleading in silence. This wasn't a storm. It was a calamity. One hailstone alone could kill the unsheltered boy if his head were unprotected.

Someone was pulling on her arm. It was Gussie, screaming at the top of her voice, trying to make herself heard above the roar.

'Butch! Butch! Butch! Butch!'

'Yes, dear. Yes, dear.'

Miss Godwin did not know what to do.

When the rain began Frank Tobias was caught at the far end of the township, at Rickard's place, trying to drive the cows to the barn. The calves and the bull he had to forget. They had to care for themselves. But the cows in milk were the providers for everyone in the town, for the babies and the children. They

53

were almost as precious to the town as human life itself. He couldn't drive them to the barn. They wouldn't go. In the evening at milking-time they made their way of their own accord. In the middle of the day they dodged him and he couldn't catch them. He didn't know them by name. They didn't trust him.

The heavens split apart and rain and hail fell from the clouds. A mighty wind roared up the valley, and sheets of iron were blasted from rooftops. Chimneys collapsed. Outbuildings vanished. Trees split like stick, and Frank Tobias couldn't reach shelter. He couldn't stand up. He was beaten into the ground. Again and again he tried to run. Again and again he was stunned and driven back to the earth. He couldn't see in any direction for more than twenty yards. He couldn't draw a breath without pain. Crashing ice and water were as near to solid as they could be. 'It's the end of the world,' he kept telling himself. 'The end of the world. The end of the world . . .'

Then he knew that he must have crawled to a ditch and was rolling into it, and that was the last that poor Frank ever knew. As he rolled a huge ball of ice stuck his unshielded temple and consciousness was snuffed out.

He slid into the ditch, face downwards, and already water was flowing through it, towards the river.

Butch had curled himself into a ball of fat, legs tucked up, face to the rock, elbows held in, chin on chest, and with his schoolbag placed as a shield across the nape of his neck and held in place by two pudgy, frozen hands.

Butch thought he was going to die and he was too frightened to think of anything else. He merely existed and waited and felt the bitter contact of ice piling up against his back. He didn't dare take a peep. He kept his eyes tightly closed and tried to lock himself up in safety behind a wall of darkness.

Butch did not realize that he was a very lucky young man. The rock that had shaded him from the midday sun now formed for him the line of defence that saved his life. He was in the open on the rock pan, where no trees could fall, where no sheets of iron or debris could whistle murderously through the air, and where the killer ice could not strike him before first hitting the ground.

His only danger was the danger he could feel but could not see. The hailstones were piling up against him, higher and higher. He might be buried alive in ice before he realized it.

In the cave Miss Elaine Godwin endeavoured to face the problem of the immediate future. She was very frightened and it was difficult for her to consider her peril reasonably. She tried to argue that there was nothing she could do for Christopher, that he would have to look after himself, but poor Christopher was so slow-witted. He was a dear boy, but so very, very dull. He wouldn't have sense enough to do the right thing. It was even possible that the poor child was scrambling up the bluff now, or he could be lying unconscious in the open in a deepening pool of water, or he could be bleeding to death from the savage wounds inflicted by ice. More than any other child at present in her care this one boy was her responsibility. She had been happy enough to leave him behind because she hadn't wanted him to climb the bluff at all. When he had called she had been going to order him to wait at the bottom. Christopher, so dull, was also so clumsy. But he was obedient and courteous and gentle. If he had been ordered to stay at the bottom he would not have argued. It was his simple trust in her, so often revealed in the past, that seemed to reach out from the wildness beyond the cave seeking the friendship and comfort of her hand.

But how could she go to him? She could not descend the

bluff. She'd be blinded by water and ice, even blown from the rock-face. She'd be dead before she got to the bottom, dead before her announcement of the wonder of these caves went out to the world. It was too much to ask of any woman, to throw her life away in the frail chance that she might help a slow-witted, usually unwashed, and greedy boy.

But beside her was Gussie, that emotional little creature, still tugging on her sleeve, 'Butch! Butch! Butch!'

'Yes, dear. Yes, dear.'

'You shouldn't have left him behind, Miss Godwin. You should have made him come.'

'Shut up, Gussie,' roared Paul, shaking her. 'That's not fair. It's not Miss Godwin's fault. No one could do anything out there. Not even a man.'

'I bet Butch's father would. He'd go. And I'd go, too, if I was strong enough. And stop shaking me. And stop shouting at me. You're a scaredy-cat. That's what you are. You're big enough, even if Miss Godwin isn't.'

'Augusta,' cried the schoolmistress angrily, 'you are not to address your brother like that. And not one of you is to leave this cave until the storm is over. I absolutely forbid any move towards the entrance. You're to get back out of the wind and the wet. I've enough worry without the rest of you catching chills.' Exhausted by the effort of making herself heard and by her distress, she waved them back inside.

Adrian yelled at her, 'You're coming, too, Miss Godwin?'

She shook her head. 'On your honours,' she screamed. 'No one to leave. Now *go!*'

She sat where she was, worn out, hoarse, her throat raw, her head ringing, but she summoned enough strength to gesture angrily at them, once again, and she saw them retreat into the caves and she saw the torch come on again in Paul's hand, and then they were gone from her sight.

She surrendered then to a private little weep. When she

looked up the hail had stopped but the rain fell in an unbroken torrent.

At the conclusion of the National News at 12.40, Eastern Time, an additional item was handed to the news reader in the air-conditioned comfort of a studio more than a thousand miles from Hills End.

The news reader was a pleasant young man, but he could not be expected to be disturbed by a report of a storm. After all, with equal calm, he had broadcast stories of disasters and wars. As far as he was concerned, items of news were words on paper that he was required to read aloud, in exchange for his pay envelope at the end of the week. Another storm was just another storm.

So he read it and this is what he said:

'A severe cyclonic storm, accompanied by hurricane-force winds and torrential hail and rain, is cutting an arc of destruction and chaos sixty miles wide through the north country, causing widespread power failures and disruption of radio and telephone communications. Numerous country centres are isolated, roads are impassable and rivers are rising rapidly. In the heavily timbered region of the Stanley Ranges, where the storm appears to have struck with its greatest violence, fears are held for the safety of approximately ninety men, women and children, the entire population of the mill town of Hills End. These people are travelling over a dangerous mountain road to the annual Picnic Race Meeting at Stanley. The party was one hour overdue when telephone communication with Stanley was cut off. It is believed that a breakdown of one of the cars or trucks concerned must have caused the delay which has left these people at the mercy of the storm.

'Detailed gale warnings and flood warnings for the region will be issued in the weather report that follows this bulletin.'

Miss Godwin moved cautiously from the deep shelter of the entrance cave to the fury of the ledge. In a few moments her tough bush clothes were soaked and she was shivering uncontrollably.

She was so terribly afraid, so awed by the violence, so perturbed that clear sunshine and this awful tempest could come from one sky, could exist in one world side by side, only a few hours or a few miles apart.

She didn't walk into the storm, she crawled into it, because she feared she would be swept from her feet to the horrible rocks far beneath. She felt like a poor, bewildered heathen, crawling into the presence of the god of thunder; yet deep inside her, so deep that for the moment she couldn't summon from it the strength she needed, was the spark of her faith in the good God who was with his people when they needed him. She didn't believe in running to God for every little thing, because he had given her a mind and a body equal to most of her problems. She thanked him for what he had given her, but rarely asked for more.

She had prayed several times this day in her fear, but now she couldn't. There was a barrier in her mind and it was a barrier of self-pity. She was sorry for herself; she was angry; she was resentful.

She stayed on the ledge blasted by the wind and rain, not fighting the storm but fighting herself. She tried to tell herself that the silly boy Christopher wasn't worth worrying about. Again and again she willed herself to crawl back into the cave, but she couldn't move her body because fighting against the desire to preserve herself was her love for the simple boy who was always so happy, so obedient, so loyal.

Little Harvey squatted on the floor of the cave beside Miss Godwin's tripod and camera. He was itching to get his fingers on the camera, but he was conscious of a steady gaze from

Frances and that gaze meant one thing, 'Behave yourself, little boy, or look out!'

Paul had placed the electric lantern on a boulder and they sat in the spill of light, with the faint outline of bones not far away. They were subdued and Adrian was nervously flicking back his sleeve and peering at the face of his watch. The roar of the storm was still there but not close enough to prevent them from conversing in comfort if they had wished it. But no one spoke, not for a very long time. Even Gussie nursed her chin in her hands, pouting with her lower lip, trembling from the awful haste of her heart-beat. She didn't know now whether she was more concerned for Butch or for Miss Godwin, and was sorry for the silly things she had said. How could she have suggested that Paul should go out into the storm?

Maisie was shaking from cold and fright, and her freckled face had gone very pale. Adrian wondered what she was thinking, because she looked bloodless in the eerie light of the lantern. He was even startled himself when Paul suddenly said, 'She's been gone long enough.'

'Yes,' said Adrian, 'but you know Miss Godwin. She wouldn't do anything silly.'

'I don't know about that. I think one of us should go and see.'

'Go together if you like.'

'Righto.'

'Yes,' said Frances. 'Go together. Then you'll each be on your honour.'

'And leave us here?' wailed Maisie. 'By ourselves? In the dark?'

'We're not taking the torch, stupid. Come on, Paul. We've got to get her back in here. She's awfully thin, you know. We're not the ones that'll catch cold. Silly her sitting out there waiting for Butch. Butch hasn't got many brains, but he's not that dumb. He won't try to climb the bluff.'

'Can I come, too?' squeaked Harvey.

'You stay where you are,' growled Paul. 'Someone's got to look after the girls.'

Harvey thought about it for a moment, and it was a compliment that pleased him. He folded his arms and looked as important as an Indian chieftain.

Paul and Adrian groped towards the gloomy light. It was always easier to fumble towards the light than away from it and Paul ran the string lightly through his fingers to ensure that they came out to the right entrance. He noticed that the string was damp and that the floor of the cave was wet and occasionally they stepped into puddles that had not been there a few minutes ago. He didn't like it. He had been in here before, in dry weather, when water had started flowing. If it could flow in dry weather it could gush in a storm.

Suddenly the storm was in front of them, just as it had been before, like an endless block of frosted glass that was breaking all the time and spraying fragments from its edge. They were not fragments of ice now, but gusts of stinging rain, that blew far back into the entrance cave.

'*Where is she?*'

It was Adrian's shout and Adrian's fingers that dug into Paul's arm.

They battled farther into the wet and the wind, but she wasn't there, and Paul pointed. Through the melting hail that was still six inches deep was one almost clear patch. Miss Godwin had gone over the side.

The two boys clung to each other in an emotion that was nothing less than horror. She couldn't have fallen; she couldn't have been blown, because the wind had been driving into her face. Miss Godwin had gone over the side deliberately.

CHAPTER SIX

The Hours of Terror

ADRIAN and Paul stumbled away from the storm, back along the string, round the twists and turns, until they floundered into the big cave, breathless and speechless, but they didn't need to speak a word.

If they had stopped to think they might have contrived to break the news gently. If they had paused only for a few moments before rushing into that inner cave they might have prevented the scene that followed. Gussie instantly burst into tears. Before she heard anything she was shaking with sobs. She knew. No one had to tell her. Gussie's intuition was frightening, because it was invariably right. She never bothered to think in a crisis. She didn't need to.

It was Frances who calmed her, even calmed them all, even Adrian and Paul, by putting a motherly arm round Gussie's shoulders and declaring, 'Things are often not as bad as they seem. That's something my mother always says. What possible use can we be to anyone if we behave like a lot of silly people?'

She compelled them to think about it because she had sounded so motherly and so wise. She didn't seem in the least frightened. She was, terribly so, but no one knew.

'You're right,' said Paul. 'Getting panicky isn't going to help. Whatever we do we've got to keep our heads. We're on our own. Miss Godwin's gone. She's the one that's in danger. Not us.'

'She's gone down the cliff,' said Adrian, 'to get Butch, I suppose. It was an awfully brave thing to do.'

'But an awfully silly thing,' said Frances, 'and you boys are not to get the idea that you're to go after her.'

Adrian buried his face in his hands. 'But we've got to, don't you see?'

'I don't see,' said Frances. 'That's what she meant when she forbade you to go into the storm.'

'That was different.'

'It wasn't different at all. She put you on your honour and we all gave her our honour.'

'It's Gussie's fault,' squeaked Harvey. 'She's the one who made the fuss.'

'It wasn't my fault. I – I couldn't help it. I – I didn't want anything to happen to Butch.'

'Girls,' snorted Harvey. 'That's what my dad says – *women*!'

'But what are we going to do?' asked Maisie.

Paul and Adrian both shrugged. They didn't know. Neither did Frances.

They sat down again and when Paul put his hand out behind him he was sure he touched water. He felt nervously with his fingers and he was right. A little stream of water was trickling into the cave.

He heard Gussie sniffing quietly, trying to hold back her tears.

On the face of the bluff, Miss Godwin clung to an outcrop of rock, fighting for breath and for the courage to go on. Her fingers were numb, her feet were numb, and she was so very, very weak.

She was afraid to look up and afraid to look down. She didn't know where she was, but she realized that this outcrop was the difference between life and death, that if she had not found it her body would already be broken on the rocks beneath. And she knew something more. Never, never, could she climb back up again. She didn't know where to climb. She didn't know how she had come to be here. She had to continue going down or slowly lose consciousness and die when she fell. These thoughts were not crystal clear. They were like dreams in her exhausted mind and she had to battle to hold on to them. Her only real desire was to give up, to fall and have done with it all.

She clung to her rock, groaning, panting, enduring the blows of wind and rain, feeling rather than thinking that it might have been a tragic way to die, an awful way to die, but still noble. It was a hero's death. Only a hero or a fool would have tried. Perhaps, then, it was a fool's death.

What a terrible thing! Not a fool! Not the wise Miss Elaine Godwin, not the brave Miss Godwin. She couldn't be a simple fool.

They'd say she'd thrown her life away. They'd say she'd tried to be a heroine but should have known she wasn't strong enough. They'd say you'd think God would have looked after such a frail little woman. Makes you wonder, some of them would say, whether there is a God?

She clung to her rock and at last began to pray, fighting against her exhaustion to frame the thoughts.

Slowly she became aware of the details of the bluff. The storm, instead of a nameless force pounding against her, became what it was – only water and wind, enemies that she could defeat. Finally, she looked down, through eyelids slitted against the blast. At the foot of the bluff, thirty or forty feet beneath her, a vast drift of wind-driven hail had piled up like a carpet of snow. Then she fell.

Her scream was never heard by a living soul. She felt nothing except the awful convulsion of her heart and a momentary impression of space and a deep sadness that God hadn't answered her.

Suddenly, she seemed to be suffocating and she believed it was the moment of death. She didn't fight. She surrendered limply.

Gradually, she realized that something strange had happened. The storm was still with her, with all its violence and coldness. The bluff was still there too, and so were the hailstones, and so was she.

She was alive, buried to the hips in crumbling hailstones. She wept a little and said, 'Thank you, thank you, thank you', and struggled out of the hailstones, down a slope of melting ice to the desolate rock pan.

She was unhurt, not even her clothes were torn. 'Thank you,' she said aloud, her head bowed into the storm. 'I shall manage on my own now, thank you.'

Then she staggered through the boulders and the gaps, through deepening pools and runnels, bent almost double, searching for Christopher, calling for him, apparently not aware that the water was becoming deeper and everywhere was flowing across the rock pan towards the tormented river. It still crashed from the skies and showered in cascades from the bluff. The skies were not clouds. They were an ocean falling.

Hills End groaned and swayed beneath the assault of the storm. Littered across the flats were rooftops and walls and fowlhouses and crushed water-tanks, fabrics and sodden paper, and creeping towards them was the swirling, muddied River Magnus, every second rising higher, reaching farther, every second destroying more and more.

The deserted little town had no one to hold it together, to help it to face its most dangerous hours. Piece by piece it broke away and no one was there to pull it together again, to nail it down, to strengthen it with bolts, to secure it to its mother Earth with ropes and cables. No one was there to barricade the broken doors and windows. No one was there to save the things that people valued more than money, books and pictures and rocking chairs and instruments to make music. No one was there to comfort the terrified animals or the little birds in aviaries.

No one was there. Not even Frank Tobias.

Paul was restless and succeeded for several minutes in hiding the water that was entering the cave. He had a suspicion that Adrian had noticed it, because Adrian was very jumpy, and Adrian indeed had known as soon as Paul had known. He had feared this from the moment the rain had started. Every boy knew that the caves sometimes ran high with water, not high enough to drown anyone, but certainly high enough to give one a bad fright. No boy would venture near the caves in the wet and this storm was as bad as the wet at its worst. Maybe it went even farther than that. Maybe this was the sort of rain they had never seen before.

Suddenly Frances said, 'I think we'd better move, don't you, Paul?'

'Why, for heaven's sake?'

'Paul!' Frances put a lot of expression into that pronouncement of his name.

He shifted uncomfortably because he was sitting in the puddle, still trying to hide it. He sighed.

'Oh, all right. I suppose it might get damp down here. What say we sit up on the ledge with the bones? I suppose rain might get blown in and float round a bit. Then we can have our lunch, eh? Who's hungry?'

Adrian was very nervous, but he rather admired Paul at that moment. 'I'm hungry,' he said. 'Yeah, let's have lunch. What say we sit up on the ledge and have lunch?'

'With all those horrible bones?' Maisie shuddered. 'Not me. I'm going to stay right here.'

Frances said firmly, 'They've got to know sooner or later, Paul.'

'Know what?' squeaked Harvey. 'What's goin' on round here?'

Paul swallowed. 'We might get wet. If we don't sit up on the ledge I think we'll get *very* wet.'

'Yeah,' said Adrian. 'Much too wet. Right up to our ears, maybe – and that'd kill you, Harvey. Gee, you'd die if you got water in the ears.'

Gussie jumped to her feet. 'Do you mean we're going to get flooded?'

Adrian nodded and Paul nodded and Frances nodded.

'Right up to the *ears*?' howled Harvey.

'Perhaps. But not if we sit on the ledge.'

'That'll be right,' said Maisie, 'or the bones wouldn't be there, would they? They would have been washed away some other time.'

There must have been a lot of truth in that. Trust Maisie to go straight to the truth.

They moved their things on to the ledge and ate their lunches and watched the water flow in. They must have watched for half an hour, then Paul realized that the lantern was becoming dim. The battery must have been an old one.

'We'll have to switch off,' he said, 'or we won't have any light when perhaps we'll need it most.'

'Oh, dear!' Gussie shivered. 'Must you, Paul?'

'Of course I must.'

His tone was sharper than he meant it to be, but he was frightened, too. He wasn't a man. He was only a boy thirteen years old.

'Switch it off,' said Adrian.

Suddenly the cave was very, very dark. One by one, even the older ones, they reached out their hands and held on tightly to the next person, and after a while Adrian could feel the water at his feet. He pulled his legs up and hoped desperately for the rain to stop, but he could hear it still, roaring and blustering in the distance.

Perhaps the water had never washed the bones away because there never had been a storm like this before. Perhaps this was the worst storm for a hundred thousand years. Perhaps this was the storm that *would* wash the bones away.

Miss Elaine Godwin waded on across the rock pan, calling for Christopher, surely knowing that her voice was lost in the storm, but still calling. Perhaps she called to convince herself that the boy was still capable of answering. Perhaps she called because she needed the company of her own voice. Perhaps she needed to direct all her thoughts upon the boy because it was not possible any longer to blind herself to the rising waters. She knew the peril was there, but had to force herself to ignore it. In places the flow of water had become a dangerous current. In places it roared and swirled and branches and bushes swept from the cliffs bounced and spun across the rocks, propelled sometimes by water and sometimes by wind; but she waded on, pulling herself hand over hand, searching, calling, groaning for breath in the gale that sought only to punch the life out of her, sometimes driven into the rocks or gusted into pools that were waist-deep and more, sometimes knocked from her feet.

Her calls became weaker and weaker. Her ability to fight the wind and water and rocks became less and less. She had drawn upon reserves of strength that had been unused in a life-time. She had wrung her thin body dry. There was nothing left except her will, but she had not found Christopher. Perhaps it would have been better if she had died at the foot of the bluff. Then she would have been spared this last bitterness, which had given her extra life for nothing.

At last she laid herself down to die, because she couldn't help Christopher or herself any more. She still cried his name in a faint, faint, call, but she couldn't hear herself or anything else. She was finished. That she laid herself down only three yards from the boy she didn't know.

He knew, but she didn't.

Simple Butch, the boy who was almost as big as a man, wrapped his fat young arm around her and began to drag her towards the forest fringe.

Paul stirred. He was stiff and chilled and aching. 'The rain's stopped,' he said.

'Do you think so?'

'Well, I can't hear it, can you?'

'I don't know. I'm not sure. What would you say, Frances?'

'Perhaps it's only the wind that's dropped.'

'What's the time, Adrian?'

'Ten past five.'

'Golly! Is that all? It feels like the middle of the night.'

Paul flashed the light on the water beneath them. It was about six inches from the lip of the ledge. The cave was like a lake. Must have been under water to a depth of eighteen inches.

'It's getting higher.'

'Yeah.'

'Are we going to drown?'

'Don't be silly, Gussie.'

'Better switch that light off.'

'Wait a tick. What's wrong with Harvey?'

'Nothing. Sound asleep.'

'Poor little kid.'

'Golly! What a day for a picnic!'

'Wonder how they went?'

'Perhaps it rained there, too.'

'Could have, I suppose.'

'Do switch that light off, Paul. We might need it during the night.'

'We're not going to be here all night, are we?'

'Grow up, Gussie. You know that. How can we possibly get out until morning?'

'Oh dear! I hope we do get out – some time.'

'I think we'd better not eat the rest of our food. I think we'd better keep it.'

'All I've got's a bit of cake.'

'I've got a couple of sandwiches.'

'How much higher do you think the water'll get?'

'How should I know?'

'Perhaps Miss Godwin will rescue us.'

'Yeah. But somehow I don't think so.'

'Funny, isn't it?'

'What's funny?'

'I dunno. Everything.'

Butch had used his brains. Perhaps he didn't have many, but he used what he had. He had dragged Miss Godwin into the foliage of a fallen tree where the force of the storm was broken and where nothing could hit them, unless the wind turned round and blew from the opposite direction. There, in the little nest he made of leaves and twigs, he sheltered his teacher from the rain, with tons of wood, boughs, branches, and dense foliage between them and the angry sky. It was wet, dreadfully wet, but he couldn't have found a safer place in the forest.

He sat beside her for one hour, for two hours, for three hours and a half before she came out of her sleep, her coma, or whatever it was. When she opened her eyes she looked straight up through the gloom and he saw a frown etch into her brow.

'Good afternoon, Miss Godwin,' he said politely.

She didn't speak and he thought she hadn't heard, so he repeated his greeting. And slowly then, as slowly as her frown had formed, a little smile formed at the corners of her mouth.

'Good afternoon, Christopher,' she said thinly. 'So I did find you after all?'

'Yes, miss, but you were in a bit of a mess, if you don't mind my saying so.'

'That's a good boy, Christopher. That was nice to hear. You preceded the gerund by the possessive. Have you been thinking about it?'

'Yes, miss. I've had a long time to think about it.'

'A good boy, Christopher. Is it still raining?'

'Yes, miss.'

'But the thunder has stopped?'

'Long ago, miss. Before you found me, miss. It was kind of you to look for me, miss.'

'That's all right, Christopher. You knew I'd come, didn't you?'

'Yes, miss.'

'Where are we?'

'In the forest at the edge of the rock pan. We're in a tree that blew down. I knew it couldn't blow down again, so I thought it would be safe.'

'That was very clever of you. I do feel weak, Christopher, but I think we'd better be going. We must tell Mr Tobias what has happened. He'll be able to rescue the others. They must not come down without ropes to steady them. Will you be able to help me along?'

'Of course, miss. Do you want to go now, in the rain?'

'We must, mustn't we?'

'I suppose so, miss.'

She squeezed his arm. 'Thank you for saving my life, Christopher. You know you've saved my life, don't you?'

'Yes, miss, and I'm so proud.'

'You're a dear boy and a very clever boy. Will you help me now?'

'Follow me, miss. We'll have to crawl to get out.'

She rolled over and made to follow him and then she saw his bare feet. 'Christopher,' she cried. 'Your new shoes – what have you done with them?'

He stopped and hung his head. 'I've lost them, miss.'

'Oh, what a shame! I must buy you another pair ... You will let me, won't you?'

'Yes, miss.'

'And you were going to walk all that way without shoes? And with feet so tender?'

'I'm still going to, miss. We've got to get the ropes.'

'You're a brave boy, Christopher, as well as a good boy.'

They crawled out into the open and the wind had dropped and the rain was slackening. Miss Godwin looked back across the rock pan and it was like a river, a vast, boulder-studded river, and countless tons of water crashed down the face of the bluff in foaming cascades.

It was terrifying, and she was sure the children were drowned, because she had forbidden them to leave the caves.

Butch took her arm and they hobbled away into the shattered forest back towards Hills End.

CHAPTER SEVEN

In the Morning

FRANCES felt bruised. A long time ago she had been kicked by a horse. That was how it felt now all down one side of her. She wasn't shivering, but she was very cold.

She was sure it must be morning because she had been lying on this shelf of rock for such a long, long time. It was the longest night of her life. So awfully long.

Everything was dark, almost silent, but not quite. She could hear water dripping, splashing, gurgling, but she had become so accustomed to those sounds that she had to listen hard to hear them. And then there were the sounds of breathing close by, the deep and slow breathing of young people asleep. So they had slept, after all. She had slept herself, an hour here and an hour there.

But surely it was morning.

Slowly she sat up and reached her arm over the side of the ledge and swung it back and forth, but couldn't touch the water. It seemed that they weren't going to drown. The water was subsiding. It might even have gone from the cave completely.

'Is anyone awake?' she asked quietly, and someone sighed.

'Is that you, Frances?'

'Yes, Paul. It's morning, I think, and the water's gone down.'

Paul, too, sat up and reached for Miss Godwin's torch. 'Cold, isn't it?' He switched the light on and played it over the cave and the others began to stir.

'Whassup?'

'What's happening?'

'Who's that?'

'The water's gone,' said Paul. 'We can get out.'

Adrian sat up groaning and panting and blinking stupidly at his watch. Adrian was never at his best first thing in the morning. He shook his watch and listened to it.

'Oh crumbs!' he groaned. 'I forgot to wind it ... It's morning, is it?'

'We think so, but now we don't know,' Paul answered impatiently. 'Surely you could have remembered to wind your watch!'

'Surely you could have remembered to remind me!'

'We can find out very easily,' said Frances. 'Just collect our things and go out to the entrance. We'll know if it's daylight soon enough.'

'I'm hungry,' said Harvey. 'Who's got something to eat?'

Gussie sniffed. 'You've eaten almost everything already, you little pig.'

'I'm a growing boy,' said Harvey.

'You ought to be, the way you eat.'

'Righto,' said Paul. 'Frances has the right idea. Let's take a look at the sun. We've got to think about getting home. Our mums and dads will be pretty anxious.'

'They'll be out looking for us, most likely.'

'Yeah. It must be early or they'd be here by now. Perhaps the sun's not up.'

'They know where we are, anyway. Miss Godwin will see to that. Gee, I suppose it's been exciting, really.'

'Suppose it has. But I'm glad it's over, aren't you?'

'In a way. I'm sure ready for some breakfast.'

'You've got five miles to walk before breakfast.'

'You would rake that up, wouldn't you?'

'Everybody got everything?'

'I think so. You've got Miss Godwin's stuff, have you, Paul?'

'Yep.'

'Well, I suppose we'll be back in a day or so to take the photographs. We'll have to ask Miss Godwin to organize it on a schoolday.'

'Can't say I want to come back again, ever. I've had enough of this place . . . Whose school-bag is that?'

'Mine. I hadn't forgotten it.'

'Righto. I'll go in front with the torch. The rest of you string along behind. And bung Harvey in the middle. We don't want to lose him.'

'Hey! What do you think I am? A baby?'

'You said it. I didn't.'

'You'd better hurry. That torch is getting weak.'

'Call me a baby! I'll give you a black eye, Paul.'

'Don't be silly. You couldn't reach that high. And pipe down, Junior. You're a disturbing influence.'

'Can you find Miss Godwin's string, Paul?'

'I'm blowed if I can. We'll have to take pot luck, I think. The string has been washed away or broken or something.'

'Take pot luck then, or we'll be left in the dark. I wouldn't give that torch another minute.'

'I don't know,' said Gussie, 'and they say that *girls* are talkative.'

'That's why we're talking. To keep you quiet.'

'I'd say that was the way, Paul. Down there.'

'So would I. Still a lot of water about, isn't there?'

'If we don't get any more than wet feet we can't complain. You girls all right back there?'

'Of *course* we are. Do you think we're silly?'

'All girls are silly.'

'You keep out of it, Harvey, or you'll get your ears slapped.'

'My dad always says – *ow!* You *beast*, Gussie. You only hit me because you know I'm not allowed to hit a girl.'

'I see daylight.'

'Where?'

'Switch your torch off, Paul.'

'Golly! It's sunlight, too.'

'Have we been sitting in the cold when it's lovely and warm outside?'

'Sunlight!'

'What's wrong?'

'If it's daylight why haven't they come for us?'

'Hurry up. Let's get out.'

'Gosh! It's great to breathe fresh air again. Isn't it beautiful?'

'Is it? I want to know why they haven't come for us.'

'The sun's high. Must have been up for two or three hours. Must be eight o'clock.'

'Yeah. Eight o'clock.'

'Set your watch, Adrian.'

'It's funny that they haven't come for us.'

'Look! Look at the rock pan!'

They looked at the rock pan, and they didn't want to talk any more. They all felt very weak and very frightened.

The rock pan was like a great river in flood, littered with

uprooted trees that must have come for miles and with all sorts of rubbish. It seemed that half the forest must have been washed from the mountains. They couldn't even begin to comprehend it. It was something that they had never seen before and probably would never see again. They couldn't even describe it to themselves, couldn't find words to express the degree of destruction.

'Oh dear!' whispered Gussie.

'Isn't it *terrible*?'

The lovely world they had known had gone, and Adrian buried his face in his hands – that way of his of expressing horror.

'Miss Godwin,' he breathed, 'and Butch! They'll be dead. That's why no one's come. They mightn't even know about us.'

'Even if they did know,' Paul tried to say calmly, 'they couldn't come, could they?'

'But Butch and Miss Godwin are dead.'

'We can't say that for sure.'

Gussie began to cry and Maisie tried to comfort her and started crying herself, and Frances, not as unkind as she seemed to be, snapped, 'Stop your blubbering.'

'It's all right for you, Frances. You're big.'

'Do as I say. Stop blubbering!'

They wiped their eyes on the backs of their hands, but both seemed to shrink a little in size.

'Well,' said Frances to the boys, 'who's in charge?'

'What on earth do you mean?'

'Just what I said, Paul. We've got to have a leader. I think we're going to need one.'

'I – I don't know that I follow you, Frances?'

'It's plain enough, Paul,' sighed Adrian. 'We're in a bit of a pickle. We need someone to give the orders. Frances means, I think, that we've got to behave ourselves like soldiers.'

'Something like that. You do know what I mean, Paul, so don't be difficult. Do I have to say it aloud?'

No. She didn't need to say it. Paul could see it. Adrian could see it. Perhaps the younger ones could see it, too. Unless they were very brave and very careful they would never cross to the other side of the rock pan alive.

'All right, then,' said Paul. 'Who's it to be? Not me. I don't want the job.'

'Nor me either,' said Adrian.

'That only leaves Harvey,' said Frances, 'and you couldn't ask it of him.'

'It leaves you, doesn't it? It was your idea.'

'That's silly,' said Frances. 'It's not a job for a girl. What would everyone say? I think Adrian should be the leader. He's the oldest.'

Paul scowled. 'I wouldn't obey any of his orders. There's only one boy I'd ever obey and that's Peter Matheson. He's got sense, he has.'

'But Peter's not here. He went to the picnic.'

Adrian had his face in his hands again. 'Paul's right, Frances. Peter's class captain. He has lots of sense and I haven't. That's why he's captain and I'm not.'

'We are being honest, aren't we?'

Frances frowned. 'Don't be cruel, Paul. I know none of us are leaders, really. You've never been captain of the boys and I've never been captain of the girls, but I think we did pretty well last night in there. We kept our heads. If we'd got panicky we might have drowned.'

'Righto,' said Paul. 'We won't have a leader at all. Six heads are better than one.'

'I don't know,' said Frances. 'I'd feel better if someone were in charge.'

Maisie sighed from the background. 'We won't get a leader this way. All we'll get is a fight. And you know what

I think? I think we should sit here and wait for help to come, or wait for the waters to go down, anyway, and then walk across in peace and quiet without any arguments.'

She was so right. Even Frances hadn't thought of that.

'What did I tell you?' said Paul. 'Six heads are better than one.'

'I haven't got six heads,' said Maisie.

The sun climbed higher and higher through the long and hot hours of the morning. The sky was so clear and so blue that it seemed impossible for yesterday to have been real. The great rock valley in front of them was filled with shimmering vapours and steam, but the water still flowed from the mountains, and although they watched the forest fringe half a mile away not a living thing stirred. There were no distant whistles or cooees. They could have been the last people on the face of the earth.

Why hadn't anyone come from Hills End? It was eerie, this silence, through the long, long hours of the morning.

Sometimes they talked about things that didn't matter, but most of the time they sat tensely, straining their ears, and always waiting.

Even the older ones began to feel younger and younger, smaller and smaller. Even Paul, who tried so hard to be a man, began to think how marvellous it would be if his father appeared at the edge of the forest to wave his familiar wave. Paul was hurt that his father hadn't come. Why hadn't he come? Why hadn't he tried? Poor little Gussie! He knew what she'd be thinking. She'd be wanting her father, too. She thought he was the most wonderful man in the whole wide world. She'd be so terribly hurt to think that he had failed her.

And they were getting hungrier and hungrier and Harvey was bothering them all the time for something to eat. They just couldn't make him understand that he had to wait.

Harvey argued that he'd rather be hungry later than hungry now. In the end they gave way and ate what they had, which was very little, and perhaps it was the wisest thing to do. At least once the food was gone they couldn't think about, or want it, and Harvey had to stop nagging.

At about midday the water was still rushing across the rock pan and still no one from the township had appeared at the forest fringe. They didn't say it aloud, but they were sure that Butch and Miss Godwin were dead. They were frightened and very, very worried. Why hadn't someone got through? Surely search parties were out? Surely they knew where to come? Everyone had known they were going to the caves. Perhaps over the distance and over the rumble of water on the rock pan it was expecting too much to hear voices or whistles or cooees, *but why hadn't they come?* Again and again they put to themselves that one unanswerable question. They couldn't get beyond the question to the reason.

'You know,' said Adrian, 'I remember my dad talking one night – to your father, I think, Paul – they were talking about what the children would do if they were left on their own to fend for themselves. You know what they said? They both said the same thing.'

'What?'

'They said we'd die.'

Paul shifted uncomfortably and found his eyes drawn to Frances. He suddenly thought how nice she looked, and how terrible it would be if she died. He began to feel a little sick.

'What made you say that, Adrian?'

'I dunno.'

'Do you think we have been left on our own to fend for ourselves?'

'I dunno.'

'You don't really think it, do you, Adrian?'

Adrian hid his face in his hands. 'I said I don't know.'

Paul began to lock and unlock his fingers and he could feel sweat on his forehead. It was hot, of course, but it wasn't that sort of sweat. He could feel the fear inside him mounting up; an awful feeling of aloneness began to shake him. He looked at Frances again and she was sitting with her back to a rock, sitting very stiffly, and one big tear was rolling down her cheek.

He looked away hastily, embarrassed, and saw Maisie and Gussie holding hands so tightly that their knuckles were white. Harvey was sniffling, trying hard to be the tough little fighter that he usually was.

'Perhaps it wasn't the best thing to do,' Paul said slowly, 'to sit here and wait. Perhaps we should have tried to get across to the other side. Do you think we should try now?'

'They'll come for us,' whispered Gussie. 'I just know they'll come.'

'What do you think, Adrian?'

Adrian shook his head. 'I don't think we could get across. I still think Maisie's idea is the best.'

'We came into this cave yesterday morning. We've been here for more than twenty-four hours.' Paul sounded calm enough, but he was trembling at the brink of hysteria. 'We've got to *do* something. We can't sit here. You know what I think? I think something terrible's happened. I think everyone's dead but us.'

It was out. He'd said it. He'd tried and tried not to say it, but he couldn't call it back, and Gussie's wail would have melted a heart of stone.

'No!' shrieked Frances. 'We mustn't cry!'

Gussie shook all over and fought down her despair. She wasn't frightened for herself – not then, anyway – she was thinking of her mother and her father and her baby brother. She felt destitute. Her whole world had vanished, because if that was what Paul thought it must be right. Paul was so

sensible, so level-headed, and she was such a scatter-brain.
Paul wouldn't have said it if he could have held it back any
longer.

Little Harvey sat quite still, his eyes full of tears, his mouth
open, drawing great shuddering gulps of air. All he wanted to
do was to howl and suddenly he couldn't stop it. Frances
dashed to him and held him tight, but couldn't bring herself to
judge Paul too harshly, because she had been the one, yesterday, who had told Paul to face facts and admit them. Probably
it was best that they should get it over and be done with it,
because Paul and Adrian were surely right. Something terrible
must have happened.

She was wiping Harvey's tears away when she looked up
sharply and found that she was not the only one who had
become alert. The boys, too, were looking to the sky, keenly
aware of the sound that she herself had heard.

'It is!' Paul cried. 'It's an aeroplane!'

'Where?'

'Can't see it. Can anyone see it?'

They crowded towards the lip of the ledge and Adrian had
sense enough to bellow. 'Easy. You'll have us over the side.'

'I can't hear an aeroplane.'

'And neither can anyone else. You're making too much
noise.'

They listened again and it was unmistakable – the roar of a
big aeroplane somewhere, flying high.

Gussie squealed. 'There it is!'

She pointed high into the north-east and one by one they
picked it up, flashing in the sun.

'What sort is it, Adrian? You know all about aeroplanes.'

'I think it's a Lincoln.'

'One of the bombers?'

'Yeah. That's what it is, all right. A Lincoln. The Air
Force.'

'Golly What would the Air Force be doing away out here?'

'How should I know? I wish we could make a signal or something.'

'How could we make a signal? We've got nothing that'll burn.'

'And no matches, anyway.'

'And he's miles and miles away. He'd never see.'

'He's turning, isn't he?'

'Yeah. And I can't hear his engines any more. Can you?'

They listened again and they could hear them, but they were burbling, making a funny sound.

'Ooh!' said Harvey. 'He's going to crash.'

'He's gliding, stupid. That's what he's doing. *Coming down!*'

'Are you sure, Adrian?'

'Of course I'm sure. You can see for yourself. He's circling round and round.'

Maisie shouted, 'We're going to be saved. Hooray! Hooray!' And then her voice faded. 'Are we? He couldn't see us, could he? He'd never see us. He's miles and miles away.'

'Too far away, all right,' said Adrian. 'You know where I think he is? I think he's going down to look at the town.'

Paul grunted breathlessly. 'That's what I think, too. And it's never happened before, has it? It's never happened before because nothing terrible has ever happened before.'

They were very quiet again and they watched the aeroplane come lower and lower until it passed from their sight, until they heard its engines roar again, until they knew that it was circling the town at a very low altitude, going round and round and round.

One by one they sat near the lip of the ledge, and they were pale and frightened and unhappy. They knew now beyond the last doubt that something was wrong with their town, because the aeroplane went round and round and round and they didn't see it again for nearly half an hour. Then it rose up above the forest and went down through the valley in the south, no more than three miles from them, and vanished, following the course of the river, or the road that led to Stanley.

CHAPTER EIGHT

Return to Danger

'WE'VE got to go,' Paul said flatly. 'And no argument.'

He set the example himself, heaved Miss Godwin's haversack on to his back and looped the strap of his school-bag through his belt. Then he looked at them all, and waited.

Adrian stared down into the rock pan. 'I don't think we can get across.'

'We'll never know if we don't try! And haven't you thought that they might need us in the town more than we need them here?'

'Yes,' said Frances. 'I've been thinking that myself.'

'What could we do,' said Adrian, 'a bunch of kids? That's what they call us. When we tried to help at the fire the year before last they sent us home. Even told Miss Godwin to go.'

'It wasn't because they didn't want our help,' Frances explained quietly. 'They didn't want us to get hurt.'

Adrian scowled. 'I reckon grown-ups are a lot of crumbs.

Nag, nag, nag at a fella all the time. Always interfering. Why *should* we have to cross the rock pan?'

Frances was shocked.

'Oh, it's all right for you, Frances. Your father's not the boss. Your father's not the preacher. You don't know what it's like being lectured all day long.'

Paul was frowning. 'You're talking through your neck. If you're scared why don't you say so? Why start abusing everyone?'

'I'm not scared.' But he was. 'What am I supposed to do,' he whined, 'when my father says we'd die if we had to fend for ourselves? If that's all he thinks of us why should we care?'

'All the more reason why you should. To prove that he was wrong.'

'Your father said it, too.'

'So what?'

Adrian shivered in his fright and his frustration; but there was more to it than that. He didn't hate his father. He didn't hate anyone. He didn't want to go back to the town because he was terrified of what he might find. If everyone were dead he didn't think he could face it.

'Come on, Adrian, Let's go.'

He couldn't get out of it. They would have called him a coward, and in his heart he cared very much about what people thought of him.

'All right. But don't blame me if someone gets drowned.'

At 1.30 p.m., Eastern Time, Hills End featured once more in the afternoon news broadcast. The same pleasant young man, in the same air-conditioned studio, in the same capital city more than a thousand miles away, was perturbed enough to raise an eyebrow before he reached for the sheet of paper bearing the next story. This is what had raised his eyebrow:

'The big timber and cattle-raising district in and around the Stanley Ranges has emerged as the worst-hit centre in yesterday's disastrous cyclonic storm. Fourteen inches of rain deluged the area in a few hours, destroying roads, communications and property over a wide area. Not a bridge between Stanley and its outlying districts appears to have survived, and this is complicating rescue operations.

'Extensive flooding of low-lying land has caused heavy stock losses. Many farms and stations are completely cut off and the final extent of damage cannot be estimated. The entire adult male population of Stanley, under the direction of Police Sergeant Crabb, is at present engaged in rescue work or urgent repairs to bridges, roads and property. Further rain is predicted for later today. Contact between Stanley and the outside world is being maintained through the Flying Doctor Service radio transmitter.

'Early this morning fifty searchers, led by Police Constable Fleming, headed into the ranges to attempt to reach the ninety men, women, children, and infants marooned on the road between Stanley and Hills End. Their location is not known nor are any details of their condition to hand. Early reports indicated that the rescue party was being hampered by landslides, wash-aways, flooded streams and fallen timber, and was proceeding on foot at only a few hundred yards an hour.

'A Lincoln bomber of the R.A.A.F. surveyed the area this morning and a message received a short time ago stated that no trace of human survival had been seen along the road. Dense timber made detailed observation impossible except in the vicinity of the township of Hills End. Most of the weatherboard dwellings and buildings appeared to be damaged and all were deserted. The only life observed was several roaming dogs and a crazed bull, which took fright at the approach of the aircraft.

'A mystery centres on the mill-hands certain to have been left on duty in the township early yesterday when the rest of the population began the journey to the annual Picnic Race Meeting at Stanley – cancelled, this year, for the first time on record. Of these men remaining on duty, probably two or three in number, no trace has been found. No signals were observed. No bodies were seen. Gravest fears are held for the safety of all persons concerned. The search is continuing.

'An R.A.A.F. spokesman commented that no landing facilities for aircraft are available in or remotely near Hills End and that the landing strip at Stanley is under two feet of water. He added that helicopter operations are at present unlikely, the urgent air-lift of the native population of Valdi Island, threatened by volcanic eruption, having drawn all serviceable helicopters to northern New Guinea.

'An announcement from Canberra, just received, states that the Commonwealth Government has voted £100,000 for immediate relief in the distressed area.'

The children wriggled down the face of the bluff as carefully as they had climbed it those many hours before. It wasn't difficult. They were agile and they were young. What was a test of courage for Miss Godwin was all in the day's play for children.

They *were* frightened, but not of the bluff. Even the torrent foaming across the rock pan had lost its terrors, because their thoughts were reaching out beyond it. It was the unknown that was frightening them now, not the physical dangers before them. A heavy weight seemed to be inside them. They couldn't smile any more or relieve their worries by chattering about other things. Even Harvey couldn't summon his cheeky grin, and little boys like Harvey are not easily squashed. If the aeroplane had not come they might have invented a reason for the things that puzzled them, but not one was too young to understand now. The aeroplane would not have come if everything had been all right.

The fear was, 'If we really and truly are alone, for ever and ever, what shall we do? What will become of us? Where shall we go?'

They crossed the rock pan without harm, sometimes following Adrian, sometimes following Paul, sometimes Frances, or hand in hand through the more perilous and faster-flowing waters. They battled across like little Britons, but they came through safely because the rock pan had ceased to frighten them. They were given the opportunity to learn that fear, not danger, was their greatest enemy. If they had been more awake to the present they might have realized that courage was more than a virtue – they might have seen that courage was common sense. Perhaps they were too young. Perhaps they were too miserable to learn anything.

They struggled into the forest, not knowing that their crossing of the rock pan was something to be proud of. Their spirits were low. Four and a half miles of steamy, sticky, and tangled forest stretched ahead of them. When they had come the day before they had followed the path that had been tramped by erring children for ten years. This afternoon it was there in part only, in places washed away, in places smothered by fallen timber, and in the gullies submerged beneath streams they had never seen flow before. They leapt some of the streams, anxiously waded through some, and scouted others uphill and downhill until they found bridges of broken trees or could climb across overhanging boughs. Soon their clothes were filthy and torn.

At a quarter to four by Adrian's watch it started raining again; steady, solid rain, but not accompanied by the violent winds and thunder of the day before. Hail didn't fall and the rain didn't roar as though its one desire was to destroy them, but in a very short time they were drenched and cold and the forest floor turned into a gloomy vault that was not at all friendly. The light was weird, as though belonging to another epoch in time or perhaps to another world. Once, from a hilltop, they caught a glimpse of the upper reaches of the bluff far behind them, with cloud swirling round it like smoke. It was low cloud such as they saw in the wet season, that sagged out of heavy skies and sometimes stayed on the mountain-tops and in the gullies for days.

They plodded on and on. They knew they were heading in the right direction, but they had long since lost the old path and were gradually forced lower into the valley towards the road, to avoid wash-aways and landslides. There were times they had to wallow calf-deep through mud. They had seen storm damage before, but nothing like this. Never had such a volume of wind, hail, and rain struck their mountains so fiercely and in so few hours. Spread over a week the dry land would have absorbed the rain, but too much had come too quickly, and now it was raining again.

Two thousand yards to the south of the town they reached the road. They were very, very tired, but not too tired to read the story it told.

'Golly!' groaned Paul.

It was pitted with deep holes and the wheel-ruts had been cut to ditches by fast-flowing water. And water still flowed, red with earth, in the direction of the invisible township, ever cutting deeper into the surface of the road, until diverted by fallen boulders or snapped trees, or cascaded over the side towards the river. It simply wasn't a road any more.

Frances looked back into the south, and going uphill it was just the same. 'This is awful,' she said. 'Perhaps even the bridge at the crossing is down.'

That wasn't an idle fancy because the river was roaring so much they could hear it above the rain. In two or three places they could see it, swirling high above its banks, thick with mud and rubbish and scum, all fouled up with tangled trees. It looked like some evil red monster writhing.

'I'm hungry,' whimpered Harvey.

'Won't be long now,' said Frances.

'We can't use the road,' said Adrian. 'It'll be safer in the bush.'

'We can't go through the bush either. That's why we're here.'

'You know,' said Maisie quietly, 'if the road was like this yesterday, no one will be in the town at all. They wouldn't have been able to get back.'

'Yeah. . . . And I'll bet the bridge has gone. It took four months to build that bridge. I know, because my dad told me. He had to get engineers up from the city, specially.'

'Four months?' wailed Gussie. 'Four *whole* months?'

'That's what it took 'em to build it; but they built it from both sides, stupid. Just because it took 'em four months to build, it doesn't mean we've got to wait four more months until they get here.'

'How long did it take them to put the road through, Adrian?'

Adrian hadn't thought of that. 'I think the Government did it, but I think dad said there'd been a track out this way for sixty or seventy years. Maybe no one made the road. Maybe it sort of grew up.'

'I'm glad the road's gone,' Frances said suddenly.

'What?' shrieked Paul.

'It means that nothing has happened to our families. It means that they're just not here because they couldn't get here, as Maisie said.'

Paul suddenly felt that awful weight that had been bowing him down disappear like magic. And he wasn't the only one. There were wide smiles everywhere, and Maisie and Gussie hugged each other, and Harvey started dancing up and down, and Adrian let out a great whoop of joy.

'But there's something else,' Frances said. 'Butch, Miss Godwin, Mr Tobias – surely Mr Tobias could have got out to us on a tractor or a bulldozer.'

Paul snorted. 'Girls! How could anyone drive through this? They couldn't get a 'dozer up here until the ground dries, and a tractor wouldn't get ten yards. It'd turn over.'

'Yeah,' said Adrian. 'That's silly, Frances. We couldn't even get through the bush on foot. Maybe they are trying to reach us, anyway. They could be out at the bluff now. We might have passed them. I'll bet that's what's happened. While we've been trying to get through the bush, they've been trying to get through the bush, too.'

Paul grunted. 'Could be,' he said. 'Easily enough. We've been up and down and all over the place. We might have missed them by a hundred yards or missed them by a mile. Golly, the way things are Butch and Miss Godwin mightn't have got back to the township until this morning. I reckon things are going to be all right. I do, you know. Things are beginning to make sense.'

'Even the aeroplane?' said Frances.

'Of course. Why not? Adrian's dad would have organized it. Probably the mob was held up at Stanley. Golly, perhaps even the picnic was washed out! The storm might have gone for miles. Adrian's dad would have asked the Air Force to see if we were all right. That makes sense, doesn't it? Your dad was an officer in the Air Force. He'd know the right people to ask, wouldn't he, Adrian?'

Adrian shrugged his shoulders with importance. 'Sure he would. My dad knows everyone. He even knows a Cabinet Minister.'

'There you are,' said Paul. 'We've got all worked up over nothing.'

'I wish I could feel the same way,' said Frances. 'It seems to fit together too easily.'

'Now who's not facing facts? They're good facts, so you won't believe them.'

'I didn't say I didn't believe them. I'd like to, very much.'

Adrian suddenly had a wonderful idea. 'Tell you what,' he said. 'As soon as we get home we can call up the Flying Doctor Service on the wireless. Then we'll know for sure.'

'Can you work the wireless?'

'Of course I can. I can even send SOS in morse code. What say we send an SOS? Gee, we'd be in all the newspapers then.'

'I think I'd rather talk in ordinary language,' said Paul, 'and be sure they got the message straight. But the blooming old wireless isn't much good. The time when Mrs Matheson thought she had appendicitis your dad couldn't even get through. Couldn't even ask the doctor what to do for her.'

'It was only indigestion. She'd eaten too much.'

'That doesn't make any difference. The wireless wouldn't work.'

'Goodness!' said Frances. 'Talk, talk, talk!'

'Too right,' said Harvey. 'Let's go home. I'm hungry and I know there's a dirty big pie in our fridge.' A sharp frown suddenly lined Harvey's forehead. 'Buzz! He's tied up at his kennel. He wouldn't have had anything to eat since yesterday. Ooh, I hope Mr Tobias remembered.'

'Of course Mr Tobias would remember,' said Adrian. 'He's got a dog himself. He wouldn't have forgotten the dogs. But let's go, eh? And it looks as though we'll have to stick to the bank above the road. And it's gettin' late. It's twenty to five. If it's hard to get through we might be caught in the dark. You don't want to get caught in the dark, do you?'

'Not me,' said Harvey. 'Not with that pie in the fridge.'

*

They weren't caught in the dark. In less than ten minutes the schoolhouse came into view. There always had been a clearing through there, that opened back on the magnificent vista so loved by Miss Godwin. The clearing hadn't gone. It was wider than ever. The howling wind had torn through it, uprooting trees and snapping others like sticks. One had fallen across the schoolhouse and crushed it like a tin can.

Someone gave a frightened cry, because above the schoolhouse, dimly visible through the rain, but stark for all that, was Miss Godwin's cottage. The roof and two walls had gone. It looked like a ruin from a bombed city.

Gussie shivered. 'Poor Miss Godwin!'

'Golly!' Paul squared himself and thrust out his jaw. 'It looks bad. But come on, everyone.'

They hurried across the tangle of the clearing, and the open ground was almost denuded of soil. It looked as though it had been swilled with a fire-hose. In places the runaway soil had piled up against ledges of rock like sand-drifts. It was mud, with texture fine as silk, and very dangerous. They had to keep clear, because immediately their feet touched it they began to sink.

Then, into view, came Hills End, and the rain beat down upon the children.

Their home town was beneath them, in the valley, and they were overcome with horror.

It was Frances who cried out a heart-broken sob, and started running, stumbling, slipping, down the long hill towards the township, and the others followed.

CHAPTER NINE

The First Sight

HILLS END was half drowned. The great River Magnus submerged the flats and had even reached the mill and the McLeods' home. Part of the mill still stood, but the timber racks were down, scores of great logs had disappeared, a bulldozer was three feet deep in mud, the chimney stack was a grotesque heap of bricks, and the office had vanished. The mill was the life of Hills End. Now there was no reason for Hills End to go on living.

The main street was a battleground in which the town had tried to fight the storm and had lost. It was a battleground littered with ruins, with tangled roofing iron, shattered cement sheets, weatherboards, rafters, and sections of walls. Something crazy had smashed through the town, determined to destroy everything. That was how it looked. That was how it seemed.

The children ran into the main street, frightened, apparently forgetting that they were drenched and should have sought shelter. Perhaps for those first few minutes they couldn't see any shelter, for everything seemed to be broken or unroofed or undermined by the still hurrying runnels of water that criss-crossed the road and every path and every area of open ground.

They were bewildered. They had run into the town, but felt at first that they couldn't run any farther. It would have seemed like rushing into a sick-room, with a clatter of feet and a slamming of doors.

They couldn't believe that this desolate place was the township they had grown up in. This, incredibly, was the place they had walked away from yesterday into the brilliant sunshine of a hot morning. They couldn't believe that the hall, that building in which they had had so much fun, had stood there, where now only a few stumps in the ground and a decapitated chimney remained standing.

This was the hall, lying in the silted street. This scattered timber and iron, these broken chairs, these soggy hymn-books and crushed pulpit, this tattered picture screen and this ruined projector half buried in mud – these things were the hall. And over everything, like Nature's net, were laid the millions of twigs and leaves that had been blasted from the trees of the forest.

Paul, looking round him, knew beyond any shadow of doubt that no one had walked this way before them, not Butch, not Miss Godwin, not Mr Tobias. They would have gathered up the hymn-books and the heavy pulpit Bible; they would have carried the projector to shelter; they would have dragged from the mud the big coloured picture of Queen Elizabeth.

No one had been here. Not even Mr Tobias.

'I was right!' That was Frances crying out. 'I knew I was

right. I knew it. Everything did fit together too easily. I told you so. I told you so.'

'Ease up, Frances.' Paul shook her, because once he had seen his father shake Gussie when she had been terribly upset. 'Frances,' he said sharply, 'don't!'

Adrian broke in. 'We've got to get out of the rain. We'll try the store. It's still got its roof on, anyway.'

Paul dragged Frances along the street, and she tried to shake him off, but he wouldn't let go, and the others were there, too, scrambling over the debris towards the community shop on the far side of the road. The roof was on all right, but the windows at the front were blown in and the door was hanging from one hinge. It must have slammed a hundred times because it was split from top to bottom, and it was such a heavy door that Adrian couldn't force it open enough to allow their entry. Even with Maisie and Gussie helping he couldn't shift it. Then he saw why; honey was all over the step, honey and about a million ants. The big honey barrel that always stood behind the door must have fallen and jammed against it.

'That's torn it! Now what?'

'Round the back,' yelped Harvey. 'We'll get in there.'

'Are you blind or something? How do we get past that tree? Fly?'

Frances stood back, much calmer now, ashamed that she had given way. She had been trying so hard to set an example. Perhaps that was why her nerve had broken. She had been fighting against herself for too long. She wondered what all the fuss was about. Who needed a door? The shop front was blown in. They were just as upset as she was or they would have seen it. They were all half silly. They were still thudding against the door, every silly one of them, when she picked up a piece of wood from the road and proceeded to knock the broken glass out of the window.

'Frances!' howled Adrian. 'You can't do that!'

'The window's broken already. What does it matter?'

She climbed carefully over the shattered glass, through the litter of the window display, and the rest followed like sheep.

'It's dark in here,' she said. 'You'd better switch the light on, Adrian.'

'There won't be any light. All the wires are down.'

'And the engine's not going, either,' said Paul.

Adrian tried the switch and there certainly wasn't any light.

'The shop's in a mess, isn't it?'

'Terrible. Mr Matheson will throw a fit. Everything's saturated.'

'We can't stay here,' said Frances. 'This'll never do. We'll all catch our deaths of cold.'

'I don't know about that,' said Paul. 'We'll be lucky to find anything better. I know for a fact the roof is off Adrian's place. I saw it. And your place is flooded, Frances. We saw that, too. To tell the truth I don't think I saw a house that'd keep out the rain. It's no good being silly, Frances. Hills End has taken an awful beating.'

'I want to go home,' said Frances sullenly. 'I don't care if it is flooded.'

'And I want to go home, too,' sobbed Gussie.

'And I want to go home to get me pie.'

'You and your blooming pie!'

'Well, I'm hungry.'

'Who isn't?' said Adrian.

'I think we ought to go home,' said Maisie. 'We've got to get dry clothes and we might find that one of our houses is all right – or someone else's house. If we've got to find a roof it doesn't matter whose roof it is. Why don't we all go home, everyone, and report back here in a quarter of an hour, and then we can decide?'

'Maisie and her six heads again,' grumbled Paul. He felt

rather foolish that he hadn't thought of it himself, since Maisie was just eleven years old and he was nearly fourteen.

Adrian grunted. 'Sounds all right. Anyone think of anything better?'

Paul sighed. 'No one's going to think of anything better. It's what we should have done in the first place. But do be careful. Specially you, Harvey. Look out for broken glass and power-lines and holes, and no one had better try getting into a house that's badly damaged. We don't want accidents. If we can't find dry clothes at home there's a shopful here. We're bound to find something that's not wet. And something to eat, too. And lights. We'll use the torches.'

'We can't take things out of the shop,' growled Adrian. 'That'd be stealing. That's what they call looting.'

'Ooh, yes!' squealed Harvey. 'Let's go looting.'

'Pipe down, Junior. No one's going to loot anything. And it's not stealing, Adrian. We've got to look after ourselves. If there's a shop full of stuff here that means the difference between going cold and warm, I'm going to take it and we'll worry about paying for it later. And first thing is to fit ourselves up with raincoats. Down the back. Let's get 'em.'

Frances sounded nervous. 'I don't think you should, Paul. Adrian said it's looting and that's what it is.'

'Fiddlesticks.'

'But it is, Paul. We'd get into terrible trouble.'

'Golly! What's wrong with you kids? Go cold when there are clothes? Go hungry when there's food? Stacks of food – shelves of it. Everything we want.'

Frances was getting her strength back. 'I can't believe it, Paul. You're just a common thief.'

'Hey,' said Adrian. 'Don't get carried away, Frances. It's not that bad. The more I think about it, the more it sounds like common sense to me. But I reckon we should do as Maisie said. Go home first. Then if we need things we'll take them.

How about that, Paul? Don't take too much notice of Frances. She's upset. Say we go home first?'

'I'm not upset. I know what I'm saying.'

'What do you say, Paul?'

'All right, but I still reckon we ought to take the raincoats.'

'But we won't. We'll wait.'

Paul shrugged. 'Righto.'

Harvey heeded Paul's warning to a degree. He watched out for holes and broken glass and power-lines, but he still managed to progress towards his home at a very healthy scamper. Apart from the Rickard property, which was naturally the largest because it pastured the cattle, his house was farthest from the centre of the township. It was exactly four hundred and twenty-one yards from the petrol pump at the store to the swing in Harvey's garden. He knew, because once he had spent a whole Saturday measuring it with a foot ruler. It had been hard work because he had lost count three times and had had to go back to the start again.

It was over the last hundred and fifty yards that the hill became steep and Harvey slowed to a walk. In fact, he began to feel that he wasn't in a hurry after all. That big tree that his dad had always been going to cut down didn't need to be cut down any more. It had been uprooted and had struck the side of the house where the refrigerator was, and Harvey was pretty sure that his pie would not be there any more. And then he thought of Buzz, the little black dog that was his very own. For years Buzz's kennel had stood beside the step at the back door. He went weak all over and started hurrying again. He should have taken Buzz to the caves, but Miss Godwin didn't like little dogs that snapped at her heels. Not too many people liked Buzz for that reason. He was too full of cheek. He never seemed to have grown up properly.

He started calling for Buzz but his voice was too squeaky to carry far. And the path was getting very slippery and it seemed to have turned into a big gutter that at any other time would have been wonderful to play in, and the rain still beat down and the light of day was getting gloomier and the cloud seemed low enough to reach up and touch.

Then he heard an answering bark.

Little Harvey scrambled across the wreckage of his father's garden and scarcely noticed that the kitchen and the dining-room were wide open to the weather. All he saw was the mountain of boughs and foliage that buried the kennel and he was about to struggle into it and burrow for his dog when all his blood seemed to flow into the ground through his feet. Only a few yards away, angrily tossing his ugly big head, was Rickard's bull.

Frances had wanted so much to go home, but when she got there she wished she had stayed away. Her father was a keen vegetable grower and he had chosen the rich flats for his house. She couldn't see his vegetables anywhere, or her mother's flower garden either, and she couldn't even get to the front door.

She waded into the flood, but the water pulled at her and she wasn't really sure where she was standing. Because she was alone and no one could see, she had a good cry, and then waded back to the road, where she stood, drooping in the rain, until her tears dried up.

Maisie couldn't reach her house, either. It had moved in a most peculiar way. It had stood high on tall stumps, and a landslide, or perhaps a wash-away, had swept beneath it, un-seating the foundations, as a scythe-cut would topple stalks of grass. The house had then slid forward, riding over the foundations, flattening them, until it had come to rest half-way down the garden at a crazy angle.

She was afraid to go near it, afraid it might suddenly groan and fold up flat.

She couldn't see their dog anywhere. He was a beautiful boxer and had cost her father twenty-five guineas. She was rather cross with herself for thinking of that. She wasn't really worried about how much money the dog had cost; she had thought of it only because it was a lot of money and her mother and father had had angry words about it. Her mother had said the money should have gone towards an encyclopaedia for the children's education.

Maisie sat on a rock in the open, in the rain, and thought about her mother and father, her sister, and her two brothers. Gradually she felt sadder and sadder and she had to bite harder on her trembling lower lip. She wanted her family; she wanted a nice hot dinner and a nice warm bed and a lovely long sleep.

When she opened her eyes again she was shivering and it was getting dark.

Paul would have been all right if Gussie had not been with him. With Gussie, one was always poised at the brink of a whirlpool. Gussie felt everything so deeply. If the cat caught a bird she would weep for an hour, and once she had been badly scratched trying to save the life of a robin. Every wounded creature of the forest she brought home to care for, and buried those that died in a graveyard at the top of the garden. She made pets of lizards and beetles and worms. Everything that lived was sacred to Gussie – except flies, fleas, bull-ants and mosquitoes.

At first sight their home seemed to be almost undamaged. Trees were down; a chimney had sunk but hadn't fallen; the glass in the front door was splintered and the cat was sitting on the veranda. Why their house should have been so favoured they didn't know, unless in some way the contours of the hill had protected it.

'That's good,' said Gussie, 'at least we'll be able to sleep here tonight and not in that horrible shop.'

They plodded up the veranda steps, leaving a trail of red mud to be washed away by the rain, and then Paul tried to open the door. He couldn't make it budge. He glanced at Gussie, but she was too busy making a fuss of the cat to notice anything.

He put his shoulder against the door, turned the latch again, and gave it a shove with all the weight he had. A few pieces of glass tinkled on the floor, but the only other result was an ache in his shoulder.

He wondered about it. Perhaps the tremendous wind had twisted the frame of the house and so jammed the door. Perhaps everything was so wet that the timbers had swollen. Anyhow, the front door was stuck and he'd have to try the back.

Before he turned away he peered through a gap in the glass. Theirs was a house that had been built to an open plan in the American style, and the interior was wrecked. The first thing he saw was the huge hole in the ceiling, and then the water-storage tank that had stood for years on a high platform at the rear of the house. It had been swept from the platform and dumped into the house and had exploded its five hundred gallons of water like a bomb burst. Rafters were down, ceiling joists were smashed, plaster hung in ragged sheets and – Heaven forbid – Gussie's aquarium of goldfish was smashed on the stone hearth.

Paul gasped. At that moment he couldn't imagine anything worse. It was a catastrophe. Gussie would scream blue murder. She'd raised those blooming fish from pups, or whatever they were called when they were little. Only two thoughts were in his mind – his gratitude that the door was jammed and his need to get away from it in double-quick time.

He grabbed Gussie's hand and dragged her down the steps.

'What's wrong with you?' she bellowed. 'Lemme go!'

She shook herself free. 'I don't want to go back to the shop. I want something to eat. I want my clothes. I'm *not* going back to the shop.'

'You'll do as I say,' growled Paul, and forced her towards the road, but she got away from him and scuttled back to the house. He caught her at the bottom step and he was breathless and pale.

'Gussie,' he pleaded, 'be a pal. Don't try to get in. It's in an awful mess. We'll come back tomorrow. Please, Gussie.'

She glared at him because she was angry that he had man-handled her. 'You're not my boss. If I want to go in, I'll go in.'

'No, Gussie. Honest, Gussie, you might get hurt. It's too dark. It's too wet. Let's come back in the morning. Please.'

She looked at him warily. 'You're trying to hide something, aren't you?'

He couldn't completely lie to her, and he nodded. 'The tank's come through the roof. That's what's happened. And I don't want to go in now. My model yacht's all broken. Mum's piano's all ruined. Let's leave it till the morning, Gussie.'

'You are upset, aren't you?'

He nodded, and realized that he was.

'But I want to have a look, Paul.'

He shook his head vigorously. 'It won't seem so bad in the morning, in broad daylight.'

She put her hand in his and squeezed it and they walked back to the road.

Ben Fiddler's house, in keeping with its owner's importance, was the largest home in Hills End. Ben had employed a highly paid stonemason to build a series of magnificent terraces from the local rock, and these rose up a step at a time from road level to the big excavation on which the house stood. Two or three years ago the stonemason had returned and for several months had busied himself stripping the weatherboards from the walls and replacing them with a veneer of stone. There was no doubt about the result. It was a magnificent deception. Ben's house looked strong enough to withstand the tempests of a thousand years. In fact, the people had often remarked that Ben would need to live for a thousand years to get his money's worth, but those remarks could have been prompted by jealousy. They were certainly not prompted by any real understanding of how good or how bad the house was. To give the stonemason his due, his work stood up to the storm extremely well, and in the few places where the walls cracked it was not from any failing of his. Where the house did fail was in the roof, that one part where stones really would have looked out of place. The wind had caught the overhanging eaves and lifted the huge roof like a hat and dumped it half-way down the hill.

That was where Adrian found it, though he had known long before then that the roof had gone. He wasn't really worried about the damage. He was old enough to understand that there were such things as storm and tempest clauses in insurance policies and that all this havoc was not going to cost anyone a great deal of money, except the insurance companies. Adrian knew it was going to cost the insurance companies a packet. What it was going to cost the people was the loss of things that money couldn't replace, such things as self-respect and pride. That was what it was going to cost Adrian and his father, because Ben Fiddler had boasted to his family that there wasn't a finer house than his in all the country, and Adrian had repeated the boast at school. Adrian would never forget that day, because Miss Godwin had overheard. She had said, 'The fortunate ones who live in fine houses should remember that when the Son of the Great Builder came down to earth he had nowhere to lay his head.'

Then she had left him in the middle of his mates, stranded, blushing, angry, and unrepentant, certain that she had been cruel and nasty. He had told his father, expecting his eyes to flash as they sometimes did, expecting him to thunder with rage, but Ben Fiddler had turned slowly into his study without a word. When Adrian had peeped in his father had been on his knees.

Adrian plodded round the wreckage of the roof, not sure whether he was still bitter or not. Perhaps in a way this was a further lesson; perhaps in another way it removed the barrier that always separated him from his friends because his father was rich. Now it looked as though they were all really equal for the first time – all homeless. The finest house in the world, if it had lost its roof, wasn't a scrap better than a slab of bark against a tree.

Adrian, in some ways, was different from the average boy. No one ever knew quite how to take him. Sometimes he was warm and human, but other times he was hard and arrogant and vain. He scared easily, too, but perhaps no one had realized that until the last couple of days. And Adrian was scared now, because he had guessed, as Frances and Paul had, that death had visited Hills End. He knew that Frank Tobias hadn't gone to the bluff and that Butch and Miss Godwin had not returned, and he didn't feel equal to facing what it might mean. He still saw the wireless as their one hope, because how could a few children, half of them only in the fifth grade, possibly hold out against danger and sickness and the constant risk of injury in a ravaged and deserted town?

Then he stopped on the path beside the house and shivered, stopped by a tall pole that had snapped and borne a tangle of wires to the ground.

The wireless was no longer a source of comfort. Even if he found it to be undamaged, he still couldn't use it. The aerial was down – and, of course, there wasn't any power.

CHAPTER TEN

Peril in the Night

THE oppressive cloud that usually they saw only in the wet season oozed down the hillsides into the valley, deepening the gloom and shortening the dying day.

One at a time, from here and there, they returned to the shop and entered through the broken window, each greeting the other without much enthusiasm, reporting the dismal scenes they had found, and lapsing into awkward silence.

All returned from their homes empty-handed, except Adrian. He brought an armful of canned food and biscuits that he had removed from his mother's waterlogged pantry. Everything that had not been stored in tins or jars had been ruined, and the refrigerator, though unmarked, must have been defrosted many, many hours before, because when he had opened the door the smell had been awful.

'Well,' Paul said at last, 'what's to be done? Do we help ourselves to things or what?'

'I've got enough for us to eat,' said Adrian, 'for tonight, anyway.'

'I've been looking the shop over,' said Paul, 'and even if we take everything we can lay our hands on we're still going to be short.'

'I'm taking nothing,' said Frances.

'You'll talk differently when you're hungry.'

'I'm hungry now.'

Adrian took the hint and passed round the biscuits. 'These'll have to do,' he said. 'Most of the stuff in the tins needs to be cooked. But what do you reckon we're short of, Paul?'

'The milk's bad and the butter's rancid. Worse than that, there's no water in the taps. And the meat's stinking. Honest, I've smelt some things before, but nothing like that freezer.'

'You haven't smelt our fridge,' growled Adrian.

'I'll bet the freezer leaves your fridge for dead. We're hard up for bedding, too. All the mattresses are wet, so we'll have to do without them for tonight. The blankets are not too bad, but everything smells so musty. I don't like the smell in here. It's all the food that's going bad. I don't know what we're going to do with it. Even the bread's off. Only came on Friday and sprouting mildew already.'

'If there's no water here,' said Frances, 'it won't be any-where else, either. I think we'd better put some bowls out to catch the rain, because you can't drink floodwaters. I've heard you can catch awful diseases that way.'

'I'm not worried about water,' said Paul. 'There's enough lemonade in the store-room to last a month. The store-room's like a submarine with a hole in it, but the lemonade's all right.'

'You can't touch it, Paul. It doesn't belong to you.'

'Oh, for cryin' out loud, Frances! That's stupid. Isn't she stupid, Adrian?'

Adrian swallowed. He didn't like such a vital issue being

107

thrown up to him for a decision, yet he felt he couldn't let Paul down. If each had refused to be the leader they'd have to pull together instead. He dropped his eyes.

'It'll be safer to drink lemonade, Frances,' he said. 'And I think we'll have to use the other things, too. It looks as though we've got to make do with what we can find, because we can't use the wireless.'

Paul had been afraid of that. 'Broken?'

'Not exactly. Power's the trouble. We haven't any electricity.'

'Oh.'

'I'll try the engine house tomorrow and see if I can do anything.'

'You can't get near it, Adrian. It's flooded.'

'It might be different in the morning.'

'Paul,' said Gussie with some anxiety, 'Harvey's not back yet.'

'He'll be back when he's eaten his pie, the little glutton.'

'The pie was in his fridge, wasn't it?' said Adrian. 'I'll bet it was high. If he eats it he'll be awful sorry afterwards.'

'Harvey can eat anything – like a goat. He'll probably eat the dish, too. Anyone who thrives on penholders and drawing paper can eat anything.'

'Did anyone see our dog?' said Maisie.

'Probably gone bush. He'll be back.'

'Our dog's drowned,' said Frances. 'I don't know about yours, Maisie.'

'Your dog's probably gone bush, too, Fran. It takes a lot to drown a dog. He'd get off his lead all right.'

'He was on a chain,' said Frances, 'under the house in the shade.' She suddenly turned away, back towards the window.

Paul changed the subject abruptly. 'Let's get one of these kerosene tins open and fill the storm lanterns. They'll do for light. Much better than using the torches. I tried one tin before,

Adrian, and couldn't turn the cap. Do you know where Mr Matheson keeps his wrenches?'

'Under the counter, I suppose, and we'll have to do something about blocking that window off. Perhaps we can board it up. Something to keep the weather out.'

'I think I'll look for Harvey,' said Gussie. 'It's getting so dark. He'll be frightened.'

Paul frowned. 'Harvey frightened? Not him! But he should be back, the little horror. Why don't you go with her, Maisie, or Gussie will be frightened of the dark herself? By the time you're back we'll have some lights on and the window boarded up and perhaps Frances will have worked out some way of cooking our tea.'

Frances shrugged. 'First of all,' she said, 'I'm putting out bowls for water.' And then she sighed. 'If you two girls are going up the hill, you'd better do as Paul says. Take some raincoats – and one for Harvey, too. I suppose we've got to be sensible. I don't suppose it's really stealing.' That was what Frances said, but she swore to pay for every single thing she touched, even if it took every penny she had in the bank and all her pocket money for the next twelve months.

Mr Matheson had three storm lanterns in stock, so Paul filled all three, lit them, and hung them round the shop. Unfortunately they were not pressure lanterns and their light was yellow and ghostly. Adrian was more keenly aware of that than Paul. They busied themselves, but Adrian couldn't rise above the anxiety of being cut off in an empty town with only three weak lights between them and darkness. Paul had trouble enough trying to be sensible about it; Frances gave no sign that she had any thought for it; but Adrian's imagination was too vivid. It always had been. He had been in more rows at home over things he had imagined than he could count. He had had more nightmares than he could remember – some of them so real that he still wondered sometimes whether he had actually lived through them.

Adrian's mind was never at rest. His fantastic account of prehistoric paintings had drawn Miss Godwin into his own dream world, but he was no longer surprised by the discovery that had miraculously saved him from being branded a liar. The paintings were his discovery. They had been there all the time and he had known it. Hadn't he described them? The few little differences didn't matter. Already in his mind their exciting discovery was identified to the last detail with the drawings he had imagined.

Adrian wasn't being wicked. He couldn't help it. Perhaps Miss Godwin had glimpsed it, but no one else had realized yet that Adrian would probably develop into a gifted creative artist, but in the meantime he had to live with the terrors of his imagination. He saw in his mind the dense blackness of night now creeping down the mountain-sides, like the groping fingers of a huge hand. What it would do when it engulfed the town no one knew, not even Adrian. Despite his vivid mind-pictures he was not a boy normally afraid of the dark, but tragedy had walked through Hills End and was probably still there, hidden, waiting to emerge again when night came down.

Adrian worked hard, in a sweat and a flurry, with a hammer in hand and a pocketful of nails. He broke into sections a big crate in the store-room and dragged the pieces up to seal the window and would have boarded the lot up, without means of entry or exit, if Paul had not drawn his attention to it. The up-ended honey barrel still barred their use of the door. It was far too large and sticky a mess to tackle when so much else had to be done.

Frances, though she was terrified of the thing, managed to start an old primus stove that Paul had found in the storeroom. She insisted upon using it rather than taking a new one down from the shelf. Frances was so much the little mother that Paul had taken it for granted that she knew how to cook, but, strange as it seemed, Frances's mother never dared to let her loose in the kitchen. Frances had one blind spot – to the despair of all the McLeod family – she couldn't even boil water without precipitating a disaster.

Paul mopped up the water at the rear of the shop. It was the drapery department, and he had to pile stocks of goods on the counter and push the racks of garments into the corner. Then he placed bowls to catch the drips that still came through the ceiling. That steady rain drumming against the iron roof must have been finding damaged spots, sprung nails perhaps, or loose ridging, because the ceiling was saturated and stained and sweating discoloured beads of water. Next, Paul placed layer after layer of brown wrapping paper over the floorboards and made six sleeping bags, each from a pair of blankets, and a safety pin. That was a trick his father, once a corporal in the army, had shown him. Two blankets folded double and inter-leaved like tissues in a packet, tucked securely under at the bottom and pinned at one top corner, quickly made a snug bag that was as difficult to enter as it was to get out of. He accomplished all that and realized suddenly that something was wrong. Gussie wasn't back. Maisie wasn't back. Harvey still hadn't appeared.

He didn't say anything, but he helped himself to a raincoat and made his way up to the front where Adrian was still hammering and trying to puzzle out a method of making a door.

'Where are you going?'

'Out.'

'To get the kids?'

Paul nodded.

'Don't be long. It's almost dark. Harvey's a little nuisance. It'll be his fault, that's certain.'

Paul shrugged and stepped through the narrow opening out

into the cold. And it was really cold, dismal and disheartening. While he had been busy he had forgotten the frightful chaos of the main street. Fallen trees and debris prevented him from seeing far in any direction and heavy cloud drooped low.

He was conscious of a deep sense of misery, such as he sometimes had when he woke up on examination day. He glanced to the north towards Harvey's place and then glanced to the south, towards the clearing they had crossed to come back into town. He saw nothing in either direction at first, except grim destruction, and he had started towards Harvey's when some form of delayed awareness alerted him.

He had seen something peculiar. For the moment he didn't know what it had been, but he suddenly turned and faced back towards the clearing – the clearing he couldn't see for rain and gloom and intervening debris.

There was nothing. He had been deceived by the poor light. Or had he been? There must have been something or he wouldn't be trembling. He was shaking all over. What on earth could it have been? Hadn't this same uneasiness possessed him only a minute or two ago and compelled him to go after Gussie?

Paul was not exactly frightened, but never had he felt like this. He was far too practical a boy to be troubled by the dreams and fancies that haunted Adrian. But now he stood peering into the gloom, listening, quivering.

All he heard was the rain beating into puddles, striking tangled sheets of iron, gurgling in ditches. That was all. Only water.

Perhaps he had seen nothing, heard nothing, sensed nothing. Perhaps the cause was within himself – tiredness, over-excitement, lack of food, or his awful anxiety for Miss Godwin and Butch and Mr Tobias.

'Paul! Paul! *Paul!*'

He hadn't imagined that. No fear. That was Gussie,

screaming. Gussie, from the direction of Harvey's place, not from the direction into which he was looking. Gussie, in terrible trouble.

Paul took off, yelling, 'Coming!' at the top of his voice, over and over again, scrambling across the tangle of twigs and branches, and saw them both, Maisie and Gussie, fleeing towards him. Gussie floundered right into him, so suddenly did she appear. She was groaning for breath, paler than he had ever seen her, and Maisie was trying to speak, but couldn't; all she could make was a choking sound.

Suddenly Gussie got it out. 'The bull! Harvey, Harvey – the bull!'

Paul felt his legs giving way underneath him.

'Oh, golly!' He could only moan. If the bull had Harvey there was nothing he could do. How could he fight a bull? How could any of them fight a bull? A bull was stronger than a dozen men. That rotten bull! He hadn't given it a thought. It had never crossed his mind that such a danger could be.

'What's it done to him, Gussie? Oh, golly, Gussie!'

'It – it's trying to kill him.'

'He's at his kitchen door,' stammered Maisie, 'in a tree. There's a tree fallen there on the dog's kennel. He – he's in the branches on the ground, and the bull's there, too, snorting and pawing, and we thought he was going to go for us. He's so wild. He's terrible.'

'And Buzz is barking all the time, on the chain, and Harvey's too frightened to move. If only he could get the dog off the chain!'

'It's an awfully little dog,' said Paul.

'But he's full of fight. If only Harvey would move, Buzz'd save him. Buzz'd do it. He'd die for Harvey. But Harvey won't move. You'd think he was frozen solid.'

Paul shivered. 'I think I would be, too. Oh, golly, what am I to do? It's always been a terrible bull. Even the Rickards are scared stiff of it. Every time Mr Rickard goes near it someone covers him with a rifle. They should have shot the blooming old thing years ago.'

And that was his answer. A rifle. He looked at Gussie and Maisie and grabbed them.

'Righto, you two. Let's get back to the shop. Adrian's father had a rifle. That's how we'll do it.'

Gussie shook him off. 'You can't fire a rifle. Not a big rifle like Mr Fiddler's.'

'Of course I can.'

'You've *never* fired a rifle like that.'

'Don't be silly. All you do is pull the trigger.'

'You'll *kill* yourself.'

'Oh, for pity's sake, Gussie!'

He grabbed her again and ran. All three stumbled together, back through the rubble and the confusion of the main street, back towards the shop, and all the way Paul was bellowing for Adrian.

Adrian tumbled out of the boarded-up window and was twenty yards up the street when they met.

'Wh – what's the trouble?' he stammered.

'Get your father's gun,' Paul panted, 'and get it quick. The bull's on the loose.'

Adrian's jaw sagged.

'And it's got Harvey bailed up. Don't forget the bullets, Adrian. Go for your life.'

Adrian seemed to be stunned, but suddenly came to life. He bolted up the street, round and through the ruins of the hall, towards the big stone house on the hill, and he had vanished in a moment. Paul had never dreamt that Adrian could run like that.

'Righto, girls,' said Paul, 'into the shop. I want you two well locked up, out of harm's way, and for Heaven's sake stay locked up. If the bull comes thundering down here you'd never stand a chance.'

Frances tumbled out of the window. 'What bull?'

'Rickard's! That's why Harvey hasn't come back.'

Frances's eyes widened in horror.

'We'll have to shoot it. Adrian's gone for a rifle and Harvey was all right until a few minutes ago. Keep these kids under lock and key, Frances. In you go, the lot of you. Inside.'

Frances held up her hand. 'Who's going to shoot the bull?'

'I am,' said Paul, 'but get inside, Frances, and we'll argue later.'

They clambered in and Paul, following them, immediately checked Adrian's work on the window. It certainly would not resist the charge of a bull, but that was an unlikely event. The door was the main worry, and if the animal started tearing up this part of the town it might be attracted by the glow of the lights. The door might have resisted the attempts of the boys to open it against the pressure of the honey barrel, but a bull would make short work of it. Paul threw down a couple of sugar-bags into the honey and stepped over them to push the partly unhinged door back on the latch. He turned and Frances was there.

'How can you shoot a bull?' she said.

He glared at her. 'How would you do it?'

'With a gun, I suppose.'

'Well, don't ask stupid questions.' He sniffed. 'What's burning?'

'*Burning?*' Frances wailed and rushed to her primus stove. She had been watching the saucepan so carefully. But it was the stove that was at fault; she couldn't turn the silly old thing low enough. Three tins of stew she had emptied into the saucepan and now she'd have to scrape it all out.

'Paul! Paul!'

There was a beating on the boards at the windows and Paul

couldn't believe that Adrian was back so soon. He couldn't have covered the distance in the time, but he had.

Paul leapt into the window and Adrian was staring at him from the outside, panting, clutching at a stitch in his side.

'Paul, quick!'

Paul didn't ask questions. This was something else. Just what that expression was in Adrian's dimly seen face he didn't know, but it had nothing to do with rifles or bulls.

Paul jumped to the ground. 'Where's the gun?'

'I've found Butch!'

Paul blinked in astonishment. For the moment he didn't really understand what Adrian had said.

'But the gun – the gun!'

'I tell you I've found Butch. You'll have to help me with him.' Adrian buried his face in his hands. 'I thought he was dead, but he's alive, Paul. On the road. On his face. I thought he was dead.'

In that instant Paul grasped the significance of what Adrian had said. The mental jump from Harvey to Butch was wide, but Paul managed to bridge it, as Adrian, too, had done.

'Miss Godwin?'

'He's alone.'

Adrian straightened up, again with his hands pressed into his sides, and made off back down the street, and Paul went with him – poor, confused Paul, torn between his anxiety for Harvey and the new complication of Butch. He was beginning to understand that their isolation was indeed a dreadful thing. These were problems that would have daunted grown men, but Paul knew that somehow he would have to find the strength and the courage to face them. He hurried beside Adrian, knowing that he was only a boy, that they were both only boys. They were the little boys who had started school on the same day eight years ago. He could remember that day and he wondered why he thought of it now. He had felt lost that day. He felt lost now.

'There he is.'

Adrian was pointing. Paul knew it was Butch only because Adrian had said so. Butch was a heap of mud, clothed in rags.

They dropped beside him, and Paul felt his pulse. It was a pointless thing to do because he had no idea how strong or how weak, how fast or how slow, one's pulse should be. He did not know why he did it; perhaps it was a gesture to hide his fear or to convince Adrian that there was no cause for alarm while he, Paul, was around.

'Is he all right?'

Paul nodded and decided then and there, at that moment, to be a doctor. He could imagine nothing finer, nothing more wonderful.

'Leave him to me,' he said. 'You get up to the house and get the gun. Hurry, Adrian. Harvey's in trouble.'

So was Butch in trouble. He was unconscious, and Paul wondered what on earth he was going to do with him.

He heard Adrian's voice as though far distant. 'I'll get the gun.'

Butch was the reason for that premonition of Paul's. It had had nothing to do with Harvey at all. This was the direction into which he had been looking when he had heard Gussie's terrified call. It had been Butch all the time. Butch must have been staggering down the road and through some gap in the debris Paul had seen the movement. It had been Butch all the time. Poor Butch.

He realized that he was alone with the fat boy. Adrian had gone up the massive terraced steps towards his father's house.

Paul squeezed the boy's shoulders and said earnestly. 'Butch, wake up!'

Butch did not stir and Paul knew that he was absolutely worn out. Perhaps he had crawled for miles. Perhaps they had passed him that very afternoon. Perhaps they had been within a few yards of Miss Godwin. Perhaps Miss Godwin was really and truly dead. Or perhaps she had never found Butch at all. Perhaps he had been wandering alone. Perhaps. Perhaps. There were so many, many things Paul didn't know.

'Come on, Butch. You're too big for me to carry.'

Butch was in a deeper state than sleep. It was the first time Paul had ever seen anyone in a state of unconsciousness. What was one supposed to do? How did one handle a person in this condition? No wonder Adrian had thought he was dead.

Paul tried to lift him, but Butch was so heavy, so big, so lifeless. There was only one thing he could do. He would have to drag the boy and hope that he didn't hurt him, because Butch could not be left here. There was a bull on the loose.

Paul heaved and strained and tugged, and foot by foot, jerk by jerk, he dragged Butch through the debris until he simply had to rest to recover his strength. And now it was dark and it was difficult to see, even dimly, in any direction. Adrian, in fact, had almost passed him before they saw each other.

'I've got the gun.'

'Good.' Paul was breathless and a little light-headed.

'Are you coming with me?' said Adrian.

Paul stood up and reached for the rifle. 'Careful,' Adrian said. 'It's loaded. Don't touch the safety catch.'

'Golly! It's heavy, isn't it?'

'It's a ·303. It's a big rifle.'

'Adrian, I think I'd better go after the bull.'

'Why?'

'Don't sound so surprised. It's simple enough. I'm blown. Butch is too heavy for me. Someone's got to get Butch back to the shop. I reckon I've got him half-way. It's your turn now.'

'I don't know about that. You've never fired a ·303.'

'Neither have you.'

'I've watched my dad.'

'I've watched him, too. How many bullets in it, Adrian?'

'Five, I think.'

'Golly! Not many.'

'Dad says if you don't hit your target with the first few you're not going to hit it at all. And I reckon if we don't get the bull in the first couple the bull'll get us, so what's the difference?'

Suddenly, Paul wasn't there. Adrian was talking to the air.

'Paul!'

Paul didn't answer, and Adrian felt suddenly guilty, suddenly ashamed, because in his heart he was glad that Paul had taken the rifle – relieved and ashamed at the same time. He really hadn't known how he was going to face that bull.

He dropped to his knees in the mud beside Butch, and breathed, 'What's going to happen to us? What are we to do?'

The rifle was so heavy Paul wondered how he was going to hold it to his shoulder and aim. Perhaps he would have to get down on the ground and rest it against something, as he had seen marksmen do in shooting competitions. And he had heard people say that a ·303 had the kick of a mule. That meant that when he pulled the trigger the recoil from the explosion might injure his shoulder, and might even throw him off his aim.

He stumbled through the darkness, aware for the first time of the discomfort caused by the continual trickle of water from his hair, down his neck, and into his eyes and his mouth. He stumbled over dead power-lines and branches of trees and deep ditches in places where ditches had never been. He tried to be careful because he was afraid the rifle would go off, but again and again he fell or blundered into obstacles, even dropping the rifle itself. Then he would feel carefully for it in the dark, feel along the barrel or up the butt until he found the safety catch, and then every time wonder in fear whether the catch had moved, whether it should be fully forward or fully back, whether the gun was safe, or cocked and ready to fire. By the time he could hear the barking of Harvey's dog he was more muddled and frightened than he had ever been.

He couldn't see Harvey, or the dog, or the house, or the bull. Usually the darkest night in Hills End somewhere showed a glimmer of light, but this was a night of total power failure, of steady rain and of cloud pressing low. Paul was blind. He could have been locked up in a cell a hundred feet underground.

He groped on, knowing now that the hill was going up, that the house could not be far away. He wondered whether his voice would carry to Harvey. He wondered whether Harvey was capable of hearing anything, whether in fact that bright and cheeky little boy had already met his end.

He tried to call, but had no more voice than Buzz the dog. Buzz's tormented barks were breaking into wheezing squeals, but the very fact that Paul could hear them meant that the dog could not have been far distant. Paul panted for more breath, chewed for saliva, and swallowed to ease his raw and burning throat.

'Harvey,' he croaked, 'can you hear me?'

Paul listened against the thud of his heart, but heard nothing except rain and water flowing and gurgling, momentarily not even the dog, or Harvey, or the bull.

He should have brought a torch. This was the silliest thing he could have done – to have come without a torch.

He chewed hard for more saliva and swallowed again and this time found voice. 'Harvey! Answer me!'

Harvey didn't answer, but Buzz squealed and wheezed, and Paul was sure that he could fix the direction. Just what the direction was he didn't know, but he scrambled towards it, waving his left arm in front of him, fully extended, like the antenna of a lobster. Suddenly he realized that his path was barred by the trunk of a fallen tree, a very big tree; he knew that from the size of the butt. The diameter of the trunk was only a few inches less than his own height. That he was close to the dog he certainly knew, but surely this could not have been the tree that had fallen against Harvey's house. The angles were all wrong, or seemed to be. Of only one thing was he certain and that was the slope of the hill. When the tree had stopped him he had been climbing.

'Harvey!'

The dog again, but not Harvey. Yes, this must be the tree that had fallen against the house, if the dog was still on the chain. The fact that he had walked into the trunk and not the foliage meant that he was probably fifty or sixty feet from the wall of the house.

That put him far closer than he had meant to get. If the bull were still here it might only be a few yards from him. It could be almost breathing down his neck.

Paul shuddered and settled the big rifle into both hands and waited breathlessly, afraid to call again, afraid to move, almost afraid to listen.

He eased the safety catch forward. He was sure that was right. He was sure that meant the gun was ready to fire – if it had been cocked. Was it cocked? He didn't know, and he didn't know how to check it. Of course he had watched Mr Fiddler fire it, but he hadn't been interested in what made the gun work. He had only been interested in the bang and the gush of smoke and the damage to the target.

He had to take the gun on faith.

He closed his right forefinger over the trigger and tucked the butt in against his hip and was so frightened, so terribly frightened.

For a minute he didn't move. For two minutes he waited, counting the beats of his heart as they thudded in his ear-drums. He didn't know he was counting because he stopped at twenty and went back to one again, over and over again. The gun became heavier until he couldn't hold it up and it drooped down and down until the muzzle rested on the ground.

And he counted on, from one to twenty, from one to twenty.

The bull wasn't here. A bull wouldn't stand rock still. A bull wouldn't be as silent as a cat. Surely it would snort and thump and bellow.

'Harvey!'

Buzz squealed again and only if Harvey had shouted could he have made himself heard. The shock of the dog's response startled Paul and perhaps sharpened his hearing, because when the dog lapsed again into silence Paul could hear another sound. Probably it had been there all the time and he had been unable to isolate it from the numerous water noises. It was a heavy breathing sound. Glory, it was! It was a snorting sound.

Where?

He panicked and waved the gun in a wide arc and pulled the trigger.

Nothing happened. He squeezed hard on the trigger again and again and the gun wouldn't work. The beastly thing was as dead as a lump of wood.

He all but lost the last of his self-control. He had even started whimpering before he remembered that he had to behave like a man, that if he lost his nerve he'd lose his life as well.

For a few seconds Paul fought a terrible battle with himself. He was only a boy. He wanted to stampede blindly into the night and scream at the top of his voice, but he mustn't. He mustn't.

He sank back against the trunk of the invisible tree, moaning to himself, with a sick feeling inside him, with the sort of pain in his stomach that could have come from a heavy punch. Never had he wanted his father more than he wanted him at this moment, but he was cut off from all help, from everyone, from everything but the help he could summon from within himself.

It was a service rifle, an old army rifle, surely a good enough weapon to work, dry or wet. It couldn't have been cocked. He grabbed hold of the bolt and before he knew how or why he was doing it he had flicked it up and slammed it home. Perhaps it was instinctive movement, something that all males were born with; perhaps it was a subconscious memory of the action Ben Fiddler had taken between shots. But there was pressure now on the trigger. He could feel its resistance.

He was almost on top of himself again, almost in command of himself. His few seconds of panic had come and gone, but he knew in his bones that the bull indeed was standing there and he believed he knew why. It was a terrible thought, but he knew that sometimes a bull would stand over its victim for an hour, for two hours, for even longer. Perhaps he'd read it somewhere. Perhaps he had heard it somewhere, but he knew.

There was only one thing he could do. He raised the rifle into the air and pulled the trigger.

There was a flash of flame and a crack of sound and a violent recoil against his collar-bone.

Instantly he threw himself against the base of the tree trunk and the startled roar of the bull was like the roar of a lion. Paul heard the rending of boughs and felt it through the tree, felt the impact shock as the great beast reared through the foliage and then apparently fell, striking the earth with a tremendous thud and a bellow of fright and pain.

Paul tried to shrink away to nothing. He wished for the ground to open up and take him into depths of safety, but he couldn't shrink and the earth wouldn't swallow him. He had unleashed a demon.

CHAPTER ELEVEN

A New Emergency

ADRIAN brought Butch to the gap in the shop window and by
then he was almost too weak to stand up. Butch was a dreadful
weight. He was as heavy as a sack of potatoes, or maybe
heavier. Adrian had shifted a sack of potatoes once and he was
sure it had been easier than this.

He leant against the wall, panting for breath, yearning to
slide down the wall and sit in the slush. It was all he could do
to stay on his feet. He raised his aching arm and managed to
bang on the boards and found enough energy to call for Frances.

It wasn't Frances who came. It was Maisie who stuck her
head out very cautiously.

'Has the bull gone?'

'I've got Butch,' panted Adrian. 'Get the others. Give me a
hand.'

'Butch?' Maisie said. 'What are you talking about? This is
another of your dreams, Adrian Fiddler.'

'Eh?'

'I can read you like a book, Adrian Fiddler.'

He blinked. 'What's eating you, you silly girl? I've got Butch, I tell you. Look for yourself.'

Maisie leant out a little farther and suddenly gaped. 'Oh, my goodness! Oh, my goodness!' She yelled then at the top of her voice, 'Frances! Quickly!'

Maisie dropped from the sill and fluttered round Butch like a broody hen, peered closely at him through the darkness, and said to Adrian, 'Forgive me. I'm sorry. Butch is sick, isn't he?'

'I wouldn't say he was fightin' fit, if that's what you mean.'

Adrian was really very annoyed with Maisie and wouldn't have answered her at all if she hadn't put a question to him.

Frances poked her head through the gap. 'Paul's all right, is he?'

'It's nothing to do with Paul. I've got Butch here. He's unconscious and somehow or other we've got to get him through this window.'

There were a lot of questions that Frances wanted to ask, but they'd have to wait. From his breathlessness she knew that Adrian was upset and almost exhausted. It was up to her to handle the emergency as best as she could.

'Gussie,' she said, 'are you there?'

Gussie was there, crowding in behind her.

'Get the broom, Gussie, quickly, and sweep away all this broken glass, and bring one of the lamps to the end of the counter.'

'What's wrong?' Gussie wanted to know.

'Nothing's wrong. Everything's very much better than we thought. Butch has come home. Do hurry, Gussie. Everyone's getting so wet.'

Frances dropped to the ground and touched Butch on the shoulder, perhaps to make sure that he was real, and said to

Maisie, 'Feel around carefully, Maisie, for glass close to the wall. We could so easily do him a dreadful injury. . . . I do wish this rain would stop.'

Adrian was breathing heavily. 'Not tonight, I don't think. What are we going to do with him, Frances? How can we get him in?'

'You're sure he can't help himself?'

Adrian shrugged. 'He could be dead, only he's breathing. I've had to drag him. I'm worn out. Honest, he's as heavy as a man. I don't think we *can* get him in.'

'Well, he can't stop here. Has he said anything to you? Has he told you anything about Miss Godwin?'

'Gee whiz, Frances! I *said* he was unconscious. And he's so limp. That's what's going to make it harder. He sort of slips through your hands. I'm telling you straight, Frances, we haven't got a hope.'

'All right. We'll have to take him through the door.'

Adrian almost sneered. 'Through the honey?'

'It's to be the honey,' said Frances, 'or pneumonia – if it isn't pneumonia already.'

Adrian groaned. Really, the girl was so right. He couldn't argue with her. Trying to argue with Frances was like trying to argue with a grown-up woman.

'Righto. I'll shift the honey barrel. I'll throw down a few bags.'

He crawled over the sill, past Maisie and the industrious Gussie, and reeled into the shop.

'Gussie,' he said, 'get some sugar-bags from the store-room. As many as you can find.'

'What's wrong with your own legs? I've got this glass to do.'

'Forget the glass. Butch is half dead, like me. We're dragging him through the door.'

Gussie tossed her head. 'Why didn't you say so in the first

place? And if you want me to do things for you ask me nicely. Don't snap.'

Adrian didn't even bother to answer. He pulled off his sodden shoes and socks, rolled up the tattered bottoms of his trousers, and stepped on the bags that Paul had put down earlier. In a few seconds he was clawing through the honey, dragging the barrel and its overturned stand away from the door. Most of the bags could not go down until the door was open. He wondered, too, how he was going to lift the door from the latch and swing it from the broken hinge. He was wondering how he was going to do anything. He was so gummed up with honey.

Frances twice tried to shift Butch, but he was too much for her. However, her efforts, even if they failed, did induce in her a new respect for Adrian. She had never considered Adrian to be particularly strong. Adrian, indeed, must have been much stronger than he looked. She didn't know how far Adrian had dragged Butch, but a single yard was too much for her.

She was worried about Butch. His flesh was so cold, it frightened her to touch him. If he had developed pneumonia how was she to care for him? Oh dear, if he were really sick where was she to begin?

The big door groaned and Adrian croaked, 'Give it a lift. Help me, you two out there.'

They helped him and they managed to push it open, and despite the rain and the cold the air remained heavy with the smell of honey and ants.

Pale light from the interior spilled over the doorstep, and Frances could see Gussie tossing the bags down and Adrian, almost at the end of his tether, sticking to everything he touched and laboriously lifting his feet like a fly in a glue-pot. That for the moment was all she saw, because suddenly she heard the rifle-shot.

They all heard it, one sharp crack that echoed twice and then was lost in the night.

Gussie froze, wide-eyed, her mouth open, and Adrian, pale already, blanched even more. He hadn't forgotten Paul and the bull, but his own tribulations had pushed other worries into the background.

Maisie, the realist, said, 'Don't you think we'd better get Butch inside? Paul might have missed.'

'Yes,' said Frances sharply. 'Let's. Everyone quickly. We'll all have to help.'

'Paul missed?' wailed Gussie. 'No!'

'Of course he didn't miss,' snapped Frances. 'Come on, Gussie.'

'But only one shot – he couldn't be that straight. He couldn't hit it with one shot.'

'Why not?' said Adrian, to calm his own doubts as much as Gussie's. 'The bloomin' thing's as big as the side of a barn. Of course he could hit it with one shot. He'd have to be blind in both eyes to miss.'

'But if he did miss it'd kill him.'

'Gussie,' said Frances firmly, 'Paul knows how to look after himself – but at the moment Butch can't!'

At least half of that statement was true. All four of them crowded round Butch and pulled him over the step, shut the door again, and looked at themselves ruefully. Every single one, Butch included, was glued up with honey. It was everywhere, transferred from Adrian and gathered from the floor. The bags afforded no protection because they wouldn't stay in place. They all slipped in honey, they all wallowed in it, and Maisie, to cap their distress, said she could smell burning again.

The second batch of stew was burnt to the bottom of the pot.

Paul waited through an eternity that was only twenty seconds long. The bull bellowed and struggled and seemed to shake the earth, a monstrous animal startled to the point of panic and just as blind as Paul to the hazards about him.

The bull scrambled to its feet again and fell again on the treacherous slope. Paul didn't see it, couldn't see it, but he was none the less certain that it had happened. He knew, too, that it slithered down the slope, bellowing with terror. The animal sounded like a tumbling boulder thudding against the earth, smashing or crushing everything before it. Its force, its weight, its strength, struck into Paul a form of horror that was nothing more than a realization of the frailty of his own body. If that beast had come his way his life would have been crushed out in a second. The power of its thrashing limbs and horns, not seen but imagined, reduced him to awful weakness.

He heard the beast go, farther and farther away, battering through the bush or charging blindly through the fallen trees along the road, Paul didn't know exactly where and for the moment didn't care. To be alive at all was enough.

He crawled into the open, still clinging to the rifle, his teeth chattering from reaction, not so much from the shot and what had followed it, but from the nightmarish memory of pulling that trigger again and again when the gun had failed to respond. He was sure Adrian had told him it was ready to fire.

Paul steeled himself and called, 'Harvey!'

There might have been a reply. Paul's heart leapt but he was left unsure. Buzz's renewed squeals and barks made certain hearing impossible.

'*Shut up, Buzz!*'

That was a command that Buzz refused to understand. He squealed and yelped and left Paul without a choice. The girls had told him the tree had fallen across the kennel. He would have to push into the tree towards the kennel and take his chance on injury. He was sure the kennel had always been close to the back door and that at least should help him to establish his bearings. Perhaps he could break into the house and find a torch or dry box of matches. That might be the thing to do. Once he had some form of light his most difficult problem was solved.

He worked round the side of the tree, until he bumped into the house. That was one thing found, anyway. The tree had reached the house and from the feel of things might even have penetrated the wall. He scrambled through the branches and Buzz had yelped himself hoarse again.

'Harvey!'

The indomitable Buzz found his voice once more and wheezed excitedly, but there was no mistaking it this time, there was a reply and a sudden beam of light splashed through the tangle of boughs and twigs and leaves.

'Harvey!' screamed Paul. 'Is that you?'

'Of course it is. What are you gettin' worked up about?'

Paul still couldn't see him, but the source of the light was on a level above him. He struggled towards it, clawing leaves aside and wriggling through the branches. Then he realized that he had reached the kennel and the steps of the house, and Harvey was apparently still somewhere above him. Buzz, however, was right at his feet, hopelessly tangled in his lead, trussed like a fowl prepared for the spit, so tangled that he couldn't even stand. Far from being able to attack the bull, Buzz was even unable to deliver his customary nip at Paul's ankles.

'Did you fire the gun?' Harvey called.

'It certainly didn't fire itself. Are you all right?'

'Me? Of course I'm all right.'

'The girls said they thought you'd be killed.'

'Girls!' snorted Harvey.

'How about taking that light out of my eyes? Better still, pass me the torch and then come down.'

'I'll try,' said Harvey, 'but it took me all my time to get in. I don't know how I'm going to get out.'

'I thought I said that no one was to go into a damaged house.'

'Fair go,' said Harvey. 'I had a bull chasin' me.'

'You weren't doing too much running when the girls saw you. They said you were frozen stiff with fright.'

Harvey sniffed. 'You shouldn't take any notice of girls. I was waitin' for it to get dark, see.'

'Were you?' queried Paul. 'Why didn't you answer me, then, when I called?'

'You couldn't have called too loud. I was only in the house lookin' for me torch to untangle Buzz. I nearly died when the bloomin' gun went off. I nearly choked on me pie.'

'Pie?' Paul shrieked. 'Is that what you're doing? Eating your blessed pie?'

'Strike me pink!' squealed Harvey. 'And what's wrong with that? That's what pies are for, isn't it?'

Paul didn't frog-march the bright young man back to the shop but it would have given him a great deal of pleasure to do so. There were times when Harvey was an extremely exasperating fellow.

Paul was compelled to forget his feelings and even his anxiety for the state of Harvey's stomach. They had still to make their own way back to the shop and that demanded all his attention. He didn't tell Harvey, but he was thankful that Buzz was with them. Buzz mightn't have been very large, but he was the most ferocious little tyke, bar none, in Hills End. If any dog could put a bull to flight, Buzz was the boy. He was the one dog in town whose bite was worse than his bark, and he seemed to be the only dog in town, anyway. That was nice for Harvey, but hard on everyone else, in more ways than one.

Somewhere between Harvey's house and the shop Rickard's bull was still on the loose, and Paul was sure that it would be close to the road. The animal could not venture far below the road because the flats were flooded, and could not climb far above the road because the slope and the debris would have prevented it. Only one thing was in Paul's favour – the bull could no more see than he could – and it was for that reason that he did not switch on the torch. He carried his gun at the ready and Harvey held on hard to the dog, but they groped every inch of the way in total darkness, despite Harvey's frequent assertions that no bull could scare him.

'I don't scare easy,' said Harvey, 'like some people I know.'

'Garn,' said Harvey, 'switch on the light. Don't be a scaredy-cat.'

'It's only a big cow,' said Harvey. 'Cows can't hurt you.'

'You've got a gun,' said Harvey, 'but I fought him with my bare hands.'

'If you don't pipe down,' Paul growled at last, 'I'll fight *you* with my bare hands.'

'Gettin' rattled, are you?' squeaked Harvey. 'That's what my dad says – the bigger they are, the harder they fall.'

What was the use? It would take more than words to squash Harvey and while they were talking they weren't listening. That they must have passed within a few yards of the beast Paul knew, but where or when he didn't know. He realized then that he could see a glimmer of light that shimmered in the rain. He had never imagined that a little band of light could mean so much.

'We're home,' he said. 'There's the shop.'

The barricade across the entrance was up and Paul knocked on the boards. He didn't knock loudly because he knew that the bull, too, had ears, and he didn't call for the same reason. He certainly had no premonition of danger because he thought he had passed it, yet he was so cautious that his knock wasn't heard above the sound of rain on the roof.

'Give 'em a yell,' declared Harvey.

'Don't you dare!'

Paul knocked again and felt the sudden, clawlike grip of Harvey's fingers on his arm.

'Paul . . .' Harvey could scarcely frame the word. He sounded as though someone were trying to choke the life out of him. 'The bull . . .'

Paul's fright took his breath away. He could see it, too. The pale light that had been the beacon to welcome them home from danger was just strong enough, and reached just far enough, to pick up the white markings on the bull's flanks. The bull, too, had been drawn towards the light and it was still drawing him, because he was moving, and he was so close they could have touched him with a clothes prop.

Paul, in his instant of fright, didn't know whether to run or yell or try to fire the gun or drop dead. He knew the rifle wasn't cocked and even if it had been he wouldn't have been able to take the animal's life in cold blood. Or would he? Only one thing he knew for certain and that was the total collapse of Harvey's cheeky brand of courage.

The window entrance clattered behind him and the narrow beam of light suddenly widened and Maisie's voice shouted, 'Is that you, Paul? It's Paul. *Paul's back!*'

Paul could have died. Maisie's clamour and the sudden increase of light had given everything away. He screeched, 'Harvey! Get inside!' and slammed the gun-bolt home. The bull, for an instant of surprise, was still, and Paul fired the rifle from his hip into the ground.

The bull bellowed and reared and Harvey hadn't moved. Paul's head rang with the shot, but he found strength he didn't know he had. He picked Harvey up like a doll and bundled him through the window and leapt after him. He was scrambling over the top of Harvey and Maisie to crack the barricade back into position before he realized he had dropped the gun and left it outside. When he picked up Harvey he had dropped the gun. What a fool thing to do! He might as well have dropped it on the mountain-side; it was just as far from his reach.

He leant against the barricade, panting, unaware of the babble of voices, not fully appreciative of the danger from which he had escaped, only abusing himself for his folly. He hadn't stopped to think. It was useless trying to tell himself that he hadn't panicked, because he had. He had left their only means of defence outside. All that stood between them and this beast which terrified even its owner, were a few boards stripped from a packing-case, and a strong man could have knocked them down with his fist.

Didn't have the gun. Didn't even have the dog. Buzz hadn't come through the window with them, because Paul could hear him snarling and snapping like a wild thing. He was sure he could hear, as well, the smashing of breaking timbers and the clattering of sheets of iron. The bull must have been mixed up in the ruins of the hall and Buzz, in his usual style, must have been savaging him at ground level. Or was it the shop that the bull was breaking down?

No, the bull couldn't get through here, not through the window. He wouldn't climb over the sill. If he came through anywhere it would be through the door. The door was already split from slamming back and forth in the gale. Barricade the door!

Paul heaved himself away from the window, still unaware of the excitement all around him, still obsessed by the fear that the bull was attacking the shop, but then he saw that the door was barricaded already, that cases of canned food had been pushed against it and that Adrian, obviously Adrian, had nailed several battens across the top of it.

It would never stop the bull. Nothing short of a brick wall

would stop the bull. But he was thinking foolishly. The bull couldn't have been attacking the shop or the building would have been shaking from top to bottom.

Paul's awful tension began to unwind. He could feel his fear and anxiety easing out of him, a feeling as soothing as a cool bath on a hot day.

He realized then that everyone was congratulating him and that Harvey had made a startling recovery and was telling everybody all about it and was as full of cheek as a pocketful of puppies. It seemed that Harvey's faith in Buzz's ability to look after himself was boundless – either that or he had forgotten the dog completely – but Harvey's exciting story was only part of the noise. All of them were chattering and thumping Paul on the back and Gussie clung to his arm with two sticky hands and pulled on him while she kissed him on the cheek. Gussie was his sister, as he knew only too well, but he still blushed profusely and protested, 'Have a heart, Gussie! Golly, everyone looking and all that!'

'I think you're a hero,' said Frances bluntly.

'He is, too,' said Maisie.

'What about me?' squeaked Harvey. 'I didn't even have a gun. I had to face him with my bare hands.'

'You faced him all right,' said Gussie, 'but only because you were too scared to run away.'

'That's not true,' squealed Harvey. 'Is it, Paul? You tell 'em, Paul. I was even so brave I ate my pie. Yes, I even ate my pie right in front of his horrible old nose.'

'Yes,' said Paul. 'Harvey was very brave.'

Harvey beamed and hitched up his pants. 'What did I tell you? See!'

'He must have been brave,' said Adrian, 'to eat that pie. I bet it was so bad he had to run after it to catch it.'

'There was nothing wrong with my pie,' said Harvey. 'It was beautiful.'

Maisie shuddered, and Frances wailed. 'My stew! My stew!'

'Not again,' howled Adrian.

Frances floundered to the back of the shop and shouted in triumph, 'No, it's not burnt at all. This time it's just right.'

'Well, take it off the flame,' yelled Adrian. 'Honestly, Paul, you wouldn't believe it, but this Frances is the world's worst cook. You know, she's used nine tins of stew just to cook three of them. If we don't change the cook we'll run up an awful bill. She'll put us in the poor-house.'

Paul felt he didn't care very much one way or the other, and Adrian didn't either. Adrian was trying to take his own mind away from the awful risk that Paul had run, the risk that somehow he felt he should have run himself. He was even a little jealous of Paul's glory, but was a good enough lad to feel ashamed of his jealousy. Paul's concern for the moment was quite different.

'What the dickens,' he said, 'is all this sticky stuff?'

'Honey,' said Gussie, 'and there's too much of it to lick up.'

'Lick up!'

'What else can we do?' asked Gussie. 'We've got nothing to wash in. I've already licked so much off my hands and clothes I don't think I'll ever look a bee in the eye again.'

'For pity's sake!' said Paul. 'Surely you people had enough sense to keep out of the honey?'

'We had to get Butch in,' said Adrian. 'There was no other way. And she's right, Paul. We haven't a thing to wash in. Plenty of soap, but no water.'

'I've heard some things in my time,' said Paul. 'No water!'

'Not until the morning, anyway. Not until we can get outside. And I'm not going out there to fish a bucketful out of the ditch, not with that bull running wild, not in the dark.'

136

'You'll have to do something, Adrian. Why don't you empty a couple of bottles of lemonade into the sink? That ought to raise a lather.'

'Wash in lemonade?' squealed Harvey.

'Why not?' said Paul.

'Goodness!' said Maisie. 'Like the film stars who take a bath in milk?'

'A bath in lemonade?' Harvey scratched his head. 'Ooh, that'd be good.'

'I'll bet,' said Adrian, 'it would be the first bath you ever took without complaining.'

'What about Butch?' said Paul.

'Frances has got him up the back, wrapped in blankets. His feet are in an awful mess. You'd better have a look at him. See what you think.'

'Me? I don't know anything about that sort of thing.'

'I thought you did,' said Adrian. 'The way you felt his pulse and all.'

Paul remembered then that it wasn't so long ago that he had vowed to be a doctor. 'Perhaps I will take a look at him,' he said.

'What about our wash in lemonade?' squeaked Harvey.

'You don't wash in lemonade,' growled Paul, 'only the ones with honey on them.'

'I'll soon fix that,' said Harvey.

'You'd better not!'

Harvey pulled a long face and caught Frances's eye. 'That's really stew you've got there, is it?'

'I hope so,' said Frances, 'but I don't think you'd better eat any, not after that pie.'

'The pie was all right,' said Harvey. 'Do you think I'm a pig or somethin', eatin' bad meat? The fridge was knocked over, see, and the door was open. Everything inside it was all right except the milk, and that was spilt all over the floor.'

'If everything was lying in the open,' said Maisie, 'the flies must have had a good time.'

'Flies don't eat much. There was plenty for me.'

Maisie shuddered. 'You horrible little beast!'

Paul knelt down beside Butch, and Adrian brought a light close. Butch was still unconscious, still very white and cold.

'I think they call it a white faint,' said Paul.

'Don't know what else they *could* call it.'

'Or white unconsciousness, or something. Frances, if you're getting pneumonia, I think you run a temperature, don't you?'

Frances looked helpless. 'I don't know, Paul. All I know is it's something that people are frightened of. I don't even know what it is, unless it's a very bad cold. Like flu, only worse.'

'I had flu once,' said Gussie, 'and ran an awful temperature. Mum said I was delirious and said all sorts of silly things.'

Harvey sniffed. 'What does that prove? You're always sayin' silly things. I reckon all girls must be delirious most of the time.'

'You be quiet, Harvey Collins, you horrid little boy.'

'Yes,' growled Paul, 'pipe down, Harvey. No one was talking to you, anyway. . . . I don't think we should have a pillow under Butch's head. I reckon that's keeping the blood away. I reckon that's why he's so pale. He's probably fainted from hunger or something. . . . I don't think he's sick. Honest, I don't.'

Frances was quite sure that Paul didn't really believe it, but she helped him remove the pillow from beneath Butch's head and place it beneath his hips. Adrian, on the other hand, was very impressed and was certain that Paul did know what he was doing. It couldn't do any harm, anyway, certainly couldn't kill Butch and might even cure him. If his brain needed blood the logical thing to do was to lower his head.

'We'll see what happens, eh?' said Paul.

'Mum's got a doctor's book at home,' said Maisie, 'but I don't like the idea of going into the house to get it.'

'We'll get it tomorrow,' said Adrian. 'We might even have one up at our place. At least I can get into our house, even if it is pretty wet inside. . . . What about that stew, Frances? I'm famished.'

'Yes,' said Gussie, 'I'm ravishing.'

'I think,' said Paul, 'the word you mean is "ravenous". Ravishing means "beautiful".'

'I'm ravenous too,' said Gussie, 'but I can't help it if I'm beautiful. Who's fixing this lemonade for a wash? I'm dying to see what it does.'

'Probably peel all your skin off,' grumbled Harvey.

'I think it's a shocking waste,' said Frances. 'I really do.'

'Goodness!' exclaimed Gussie. 'Listen to her! All that stew burnt and she's got the cheek to talk about waste. Come on, Paul. It was your idea. Give him the bottle-opener, Frances.'

Frances sighed and passed the bottle-opener to Paul and apparently for the first time noticed the condition of his raincoat.

'Paul,' she shrieked, 'that brand-new coat!'

Paul blinked, taken aback, and caught sight of the coat himself for the first time. He was still wearing it. One pocket was torn and it was all but covered in mud.

'Oh, golly!' he said.

'Is that all you can say?' screeched Frances. 'They cost seven pounds nineteen and eleven. I saw it on the tag.'

'All right, all right,' wailed Paul. 'Keep your hair on. You don't think I did it on purpose, do you? What would you rather have – Harvey gored by a bull or a tear in a raincoat?'

'That's not the point at all, Paul Mace. If we're going to use things that don't belong to us we've got to look after them.'

'Golly, Frances, I'm not shouting for joy about it. I didn't know it had happened.'

'You're being a bit hard, Frances,' growled Adrian.

'You are, too,' flared Gussie. 'You leave Paul alone, Frances McLeod. You're not even his sister. You're not allowed to growl at him, and I'll pay for it out of my bank. That's what I'll do.'

'Thank you, Gussie,' said Paul, 'but I'll pay for it myself . . . Righto, you sticky people. Two bottles in the sink and you'll all have to wash in it. You'd better grab a towel each from the shelf.'

Paul took the lamp and went out into the store-room, and Gussie glared at Frances. 'You miserable thing,' she said, 'just because you burnt the stew doesn't mean you can get cross with everyone.'

Frances looked so forlorn that they thought she was going to cry, so they left her to it. They all took a towel down from the shelf, even hopeful Harvey, and followed Paul out to the rear of the building.

And when she was alone Frances did cry.

Paul emptied two bottles of lemonade into the wash-basin and offered Maisie the soap.

'Away you go,' he said, 'and if it doesn't lather I'm a Dutch uncle. It's foaming an inch deep already.'

Maisie smiled appreciatively, accepted the soap and waved the eager audience back. First she lowered her face over the basin and shrieked, 'It *spits!*'

'What did you expect it to do?' squeaked Harvey. 'Pull your nose?'

'Really, Harvey Collins!'

Harvey giggled and Maisie plunged her hands and the soap into the basin and instantly the lemonade foamed up to her elbows and she started shrieking again.

'For pity's sake,' yelled Paul, 'get on with it, you silly girl.'

'Don't be an old sour-puss,' snapped Gussie. 'Hop into it, Maisie.'

Maisie giggled and squealed and dipped her face into the basin and suddenly recoiled from it, panting and spluttering and licking her lips.

'Oh, goodness!' she said. 'I've lost the soap.'

'I know you,' squealed Harvey. 'You meant to lose it. You'll have drunk it all up before the rest of us can get near it.'

'It is a bit of a circus,' tittered Adrian. 'I don't think it's going to work.'

'Of course it'll work,' said Paul sharply.

Maisie fished through the foam until she found the soap, but she was almost helpless with laughter. She shook all over and valiantly tried to lather the soap, but she might as well have tried to get froth from stone. Every time she touched the lemonade it hissed and bubbled, but the soap itself was dead. It wouldn't lather.

'You're a Dutch uncle,' said Adrian to Paul. 'Just as well you didn't promise to eat your hat.'

Paul wasn't very happy about it and didn't take the failure as well as he should have done.

'All right,' he said, scowling, 'wash yourselves any way you please. I don't care.'

He tramped from the store-room, peeling off his raincoat and dropping it in a heap on the floor in front of Frances. He realized, as he glanced at her defiantly, that she had been crying. For the moment he didn't know what to do.

'I'm sorry I was cross with you, Paul,' she said.

He looked down at his coat and was only an instant short of kicking it when his self-control asserted itself. He recovered the coat and smiled, even if it was a little grudgingly.

'That's all right. I was pretty short with you, too. We're not going to do very well if we start fighting. Shake!'

They shook hands and laughed.

'Did you really burn the stew, Frances?' he said.

'I'm an awful cook, Paul. Truly I am. But I'll darn your coat for you tomorrow and sponge it clean and then you won't have to pay all that money for nothing.'

'The soap wouldn't lather, either. I was so sure it would.'

'We all make mistakes, Paul. We've all got to learn, you know, and from what I saw of that road this afternoon we might have to learn a lot more before we're through. Do you want some stew?'

'Yes, please.'

'You should have a wash first.'

'As Harvey would say, the dirt will give it more body.'

She gave him a cup full of stew and a spoon. 'It's not very fancy,' she said, 'but I'll leave you with it. It sounds as though they're having trouble with Harvey.'

'Trust Harvey. I suppose he's lapping it up instead of washing with it.'

Frances shuddered and skipped out of sight. Paul was aware of some slight surprise. He hadn't expected Frances to skip like a child. To him she seemed to have such an old head on her shoulders, but then he caught the aroma of the stew and suddenly felt almost sick with hunger. He wolfed it down, and was on his knees beside Butch when the others returned from the store-room.

A faint touch of colour was coming back to Butch's cheeks and his flesh was less clammy. Paul realized that if Butch had developed any infection in his lungs probably the first symptom would be heavy or harsh breathing. That even happened with an ordinary cold, so he pressed an ear to Butch's chest and listened hard. There seemed to be no rattles or gurgling or wheezing. In fact, Butch seemed to be breathing easily and his heart was pumping firmly like a good diesel engine.

Paul looked up and the others were there.

'Well?' said Adrian.

'I reckon he's all right,' said Paul. 'He might have been unconscious when we dragged him here, but do you know what? I'd say he was asleep now, nothing worse than that.'

'We'd better wake him up,' said Frances. 'He might be able to tell us about Miss Godwin.'

For some reason or other that made Paul a little frightened. 'I don't know about waking him up,' he said. 'I think we ought to wait until he wakes up himself.'

'Good oh,' said Harvey. 'Let's have some stew, eh?'

Paul said, 'How did the wash go?'

'It was wet,' said Adrian, 'if that's what you mean, but we got the honey off, even if most of it is on the towels. The lemonade turned a horrible colour. A real, dirty grey. Even Harvey wouldn't drink it.'

'Better have your stew,' said Paul, 'while I open a few tins of fruit. You'd better be book-keeper, Maisie. Keep a check on everything we take.'

They turned the lights low at nine-fifteen and outside water was still spilling from the spoutings. They couldn't hear the rain, so probably it was a steady drizzle but not heavy enough to be audible on the roof. All snuggled into their blankets except Adrian. He sat in a chair, wrapped in his blanket, on watch.

The air had turned very cold, and there was no form of heating in the shop – no fireplace, no stove – nothing except a brand-new kerosene radiator on one of the shelves. None of them had used one before and Frances had refused to permit anyone to light it. She said they would have to practise on it first out in the open air, where there was no danger of fire.

Adrian sat in his chair, conscious of the deepening silence now that the last voice was stilled, aware of the strange shadows and the pale glimmer from the lamps, slowly realizing that all had drifted into sleep except himself.

He was very, very tired, and had to fight against himself to keep his eyes open, but as it became harder to remain awake his hearing became more and more sensitive. He could hear an owl, mournfully hooting, and somewhere a dog would howl for a minute or two and then lapse again into silence. Every now and again there was another sound, a scratching sound, and he started thinking of rats.

That startled him back to consciousness, to a giddiness and a sense of sickness, and he peered nervously at his watch. Its dim face told him that it was twenty minutes to ten. He still had two hours and thirty-five minutes to go before he could rouse Paul. That period seemed to stretch ahead of him towards eternity.

He wondered then whose dog it was that he could hear, but it was a long way off, near Rickard's place by the sound of it. That sent his thoughts out beyond the limits of this cold, dark room, out over the hillside and down to the river, out over all that destruction lying swamped beneath this blanket of night. Perhaps they would walk out in the morning and find everything as it used to be – the smoke from the kitchen fires, the engine beating at the mill, voices eddying on the air, cockerels crowing, and Rickard's horse clip-clopping home after the milk round. Perhaps that peaceful picture was not a dream; perhaps the terror so recently behind them was only a nightmare. But no, that wash he had taken in lemonade had been real enough, because he could feel his skin tightening as though it were shrinking. He had exchanged one stickiness – that of honey – for another. The beastly lemonade was drying out like glue.

Then something drew his eyes. His heart leapt because the movement frightened him. It was hard to see anything distinctly in this gloom and his peace of mind was unsettled by his fear of rats. The movement had been amongst the sleeping bodies and he realized he didn't have a weapon, not even a broomstick or an axe-handle, and certainly not the rifle. That was odd. He couldn't remember seeing the rifle again, not since Paul's return with Harvey.

Crumbs! Where had Paul put the rifle?

How silly could you get? The first thought had been better – a broomstick or an axe-handle. He couldn't use a rifle in here. He'd kill someone.

Adrian was wide awake now, cold, and so alert that he trembled. Slowly he peeled his blanket off and eased himself out of the chair to his feet, trying to place the position of the axe-handles in his mind, but afraid to take his eyes away from the spot where the movement had been. He knew his gaze had not wavered an inch one way or the other and suddenly he saw the movement again. In the gloom it was like the throat of a swan. It was a hand, a raised arm.

Adrian grunted with relief and lowered himself back into his chair, with his nerves so jumpy that he started panting. He pulled the blanket round his shoulders again, and again suddenly, again sharply, the hand moved and someone groaned.

Adrian sat up rigidly, knowing that nothing could hurt him, but disturbed as he so often was by the powers of his imagination. It was just that he was the oldest person here. At thirteen years and ten months he was older than any person alive in Hills End, as far as they knew, and so he was supposed to be the bravest. That somewhere or other there might have been a dead person only made it worse. That there wasn't a single grown-up to lean on wasn't half the fun that he once thought it might be. Not now. Not in the middle of the night. Not with these vast mountains outside rolling farther and farther into the blackness, for scores and scores of miles, without a township or a house or a hut or a single living man. There was nothing out there except a dog howling, an owl hooting, and dense forest devastated by a cyclone. But perhaps his father was coming. Perhaps all the men were coming, fighting through the bush towards this group of frightened children, perhaps struggling along the road, or even preparing to drop by parachute from an aeroplane in the morning. Surely nothing could be serious enough to stop the men from coming?

Somehow Adrian wasn't sure. Somehow, a powerful doubt had injected into him a sense of gloom and isolation that hourly had grown stronger, despite the arguments that they had thought up to dismiss those fears. This misery of his was too deep-seated to be beaten by a few brave words of cheer.

He jolted again from his thoughts to an acute awareness of his surroundings. The moving arm had become the head and shoulders of a person sitting up. It was Butch.

Adrian lurched from his chair, stumbled from his blanket, and hurried to the fat boy, taking the dim lamp with him. This was why he had had to sit on watch. It was for Butch that they had decided that one person must always be awake.

Butch's eyes were open and he was breathing heavily. His expression was not vacant or afraid, but puzzled. He was peering into the gloom, at the sleeping figures around him, and then at Adrian.

'Hi,' he said thickly. 'How'd I get here?'

Adrian dropped beside him. 'We brought you, Butch. Are you all right?'

'Me feet are awful sore.'

'But you *are* all right?'

'I'm hungry.'

Adrian grinned in relief. 'They always say there's not too much wrong with a person if he's hungry.'

Butch was almost still except for a slow swaying of his shoulders. Adrian could see that the boy was trying to think. His brow was puckering and his mouth was twisting to one side.

'What's wrong, Butch?'

Butch bit his fingers. 'Adrian,' he mumbled, 'didn't . . . wasn't . . . Miss Godwin was with me, wasn't she?'

'No.'

Two big tears squeezed from Butch's eyes. 'Oh crikey, Adrian!'

'Where did you leave her?'

'I don't know. I can't think. I thought we was together. . . .'

'Was she hurt?'

Butch shook his head. 'I don't think so. But why wasn't she with me? Where did she go?'

'Which way did you come?'

Butch bit his fingers again and ran his nails across his lips. 'Where are we?' he asked.

'In Matheson's shop.'

He suddenly burst out, 'Where's me mum and dad?'

Harvey stirred and Adrian put his fingers to his lips. 'Sh! Don't let's wake the others. Let's sort this out together.'

As soon as he had said it Adrian wondered why he wanted to sort it out without the help of the others. Perhaps it was be-cause Paul had saved Harvey from the bull, when Adrian still knew that he should have done it himself.

'Where's everybody?' stammered Butch. 'You've got to tell me.'

'They're not home yet.'

'But – what day is it?'

'It's nearly ten o'clock, Sunday night. The road's gone, Butch. The bridge is probably down. They haven't been able to get through. They'll all be here in the morning; don't you worry. . . . Try to remember how you got here. We found you in the main street just below my place.'

'Where's Mr Tobias?'

Adrian didn't know what to say. He was even beginning to get a little desperate himself.

'We don't know much yet, Butch,' he said. 'We didn't get

back ourselves until nearly dark. Mr Tobias might even be out looking for us. . . . Remember, Butch. Think back. Which way did you come?'

'We tried to come a dozen ways.' It was obvious that Butch wasn't too sure of anything. 'We might have made it once or twice over tough spots, but Miss Godwin was too tired. We had to keep lookin' for an easy way. Somehow, somehow I think we must've come over the top and down the old log trail, 'cos we could see the town. Often we could see the town, all broken, all bleedin' and broken. I know we was together, 'cos I had a good howl and Miss Godwin put her arm round me. We could see her house, too, with the roof all busted and the walls down. We must've come down the old log trail.'

'But you don't know where you lost her?'

Butch sobbed a little. 'I didn't know I'd lost her. I thought we was together all the way.'

'You hungry still?'

Butch nodded and Adrian went to the confectionery shelf and took two blocks of chocolate.

'Wrap yourself round these, Butch,' he said, 'and then go back to sleep. Everything's all right.'

'Can I have *both* blocks? Two whole blocks of chocolate for me?'

Adrian smiled and felt very generous and kindly and noble. 'Both for you, and in the morning you can have anything you like to eat. . . . Good night, Butch.'

The fat boy squinted at Adrian. 'Where are you going?'

'Nowhere.'

'Well, what are you puttin' the coat on for? What are you doin' with the lamp?'

'I forgot to leave the billy out for the milk.'

'Oh.' Butch nodded slowly, and unwrapped his chocolate and for the moment was content.

He slowly ate his way through his two blocks, savouring the

smoothness to the last swallow. The flavour didn't mean much to Butch because his sense of taste responded only to extremes, but there was something about chocolate that was very, very nice. It seemed to warm him right out to the tips of his poor, stinging toes. It did occur to him that Adrian had been gone a long time, but Butch was too worn out, too weary, too sad, to do anything much except drift back into sleep.

Adrian didn't feel brave, but he wasn't old enough to understand that a person did not have to be without fear to be brave. He thought brave men weren't afraid of anything, and that they were heroes because nothing frightened them. He didn't understand that men became heroes because they fought against their fears and managed to do things that they had thought they couldn't do.

Adrian searched for the rifle and was heavy at heart when he realized it was not to be found. He could have wakened Paul, but that would have given everything away. He wanted to get out into the dark, on to the old log trail, and find Miss Godwin while the others slept. Adrian's conscience was troubling him. This would not have happened to Miss Godwin if he hadn't lied about the caves. Perhaps the lie had led them all to an exciting discovery, but nothing could alter the fact that Adrian's lie was responsible for everything that had happened to them. But for that lie all would have been far away with their parents and families. What Miss Godwin's plight might have been in those different circumstances Adrian didn't know, but it didn't really matter. She might have been worse off; she might have been killed by the tree that crashed across her house; she might have gone the same unknown way as poor Mr Tobias; but events had taken this particular course because Adrian had lied.

Adrian was subject to greater extremes of emotion than the rest of his friends. His moments of elation were wilder, his moments of happiness were more delirious, and his moments of guilt or misery were far blacker. Adrian seemed to go through life treading on a tight wire, wobbling from side to side, from one side that was despair to the other side that was sparkling with joy. He never seemed to get his balance between the two.

He listened carefully at the barricaded window because that fearful bull was still there somewhere. Adrian heard nothing, only the dripping of water, but there was a cold, raw feeling in the air that he had not noticed before.

He removed the panel quietly, turned his light low, and slid over the sill to the ground. Instantly, his heart missed a beat. That horrid little dog of Harvey's was baring its teeth not an inch from his ankle. He shuddered and hissed, 'Go away! Go away!' and then saw the rifle on the ground in the mud.

He grabbed at the rifle and the dog didn't dart for his hand, but jumped back, and Adrian realized that it was briskly wagging its ridiculous tail. Now what was that in aid of? Adrian was trembling all over, actually shaking at the knees with fright, because he wouldn't have trusted this little hound as far as he could throw it. It was a thoroughly nasty dog and about as trustworthy as a death adder. Was it afraid of the rifle? Or was it, by instinct, ready for the hunt or eager for a frolic?

Adrian tucked the butt of the rifle under his arm and the dog kept its distance without trace of hostility, continuing to wag its tial, continuing to appear in every way anxious to be on the move. Maybe this dog of Harvey's was the source of the scratching sound he had heard. Perhaps the little dog had scratched against the door. Perhaps there weren't any rats at all.

Adrian shivered and looked up into the blackness towards the old log trail. The rain had ceased, but it had been replaced by a thin mist that turned the glass of his ugly storm lantern into a glowing form that reminded him of old-world Christmas pictures. It was this mist that had sharpened the air. He wondered what it might mean to him. If it were the cloud base sinking deeper and deeper into the valley, it might thicken as he climbed the hill. It might become a dense fog through which he could see nothing, not even the way back.

He wiped the mud from the rifle and then checked it, ejecting the spent cartridge from the breach and ramming a fresh one home. He engaged the safety catch firmly, but the gun was ready to fire in an instant, and Buzz was watching him curiously, with his head cocked to one side. The gun was a comfort. It really was. It was like a friend with a strong arm.

Slowly, then, and still not without fear, Adrian made his way along the road, through the maze of debris and rubble, with that strange little dog trotting at his side. Adrian saw nothing of the bull and heard nothing of it, but not for a moment was it out of his mind. So afraid was he that he stumbled along in all but total darkness rather than turn his lantern up. Even when he was out of the township and had begun the climb that would take him past the schoolhouse, he stood still for almost a minute of indecision, not knowing which was the greater danger, to grope in the dark or to turn up the flame.

He shivered with his fear and peered into the night and heard again the hooting of the distant owl. It was an awful sound, and he turned the lamp up sharply, panting, glancing round about into the fog, and his teeth started chattering and his legs were almost too weak to support him.

He realized then, with a shock, that the dog was no longer with him.

'Buzz,' he cried.

But the dog didn't answer. All he heard was a peculiar sound that no dog could ever have made. His fears began to run riot, and because no one was there to hear him he didn't try to stop the whimper of terror that welled up from within him. He didn't wait any longer, couldn't wait any longer. His indecision was gone, but not the way he had hoped.

Adrian stumbled back down the hill, hating himself, terrified by the images of nameless perils that he knew he was creating in his own mind.

Paul sat up suddenly.

It was a strange feeling, though it had happened to him once or twice before – once at Christmas when someone had entered his bedroom, and another time when Gussie had been ill at night and no one else had heard her call.

Wide awake. As alert as though he had not slept at all, and he saw the light in the window opening.

'Who's that?' he whispered fiercely.

Adrian came round the front of the counter walking unsteadily, carrying the rifle, and breathing so heavily that Paul could hear him.

Paul wriggled out of his sleeping bag and quickly stepped over the sleeping figures round him, for some reason deeply anxious to get to Adrian as soon as he could.

'What's wrong?'

Adrian slumped into his chair and dropped his rifle. 'That rotten bull.'

Paul gasped. 'You *haven't* been outside?'

Adrian looked washed out, but his sigh expressed more than exhaustion. 'Yeah, I've been outside. Butch . . .'

'What about Butch?'

Adrian told him.

'So,' said Paul, 'you decided to look for Miss Godwin?'

'Yeah. But the mist is getting bad. It's hard to see. And it's – hard to see.'

'What about the bull?'

'I heard the thing. Up on the hill, I heard it.'

'Up where Miss Godwin might be?'

Adrian nodded in despair.

'I couldn't face it, Paul. I couldn't.'

'Don't worry. I wouldn't have been able to, either.'

'But you *did* face it.'

'That was different. Golly, that was different altogether . . . What's the time?'

'About half past ten.' Adrian peered at his watch. 'To be exact, twenty-five to eleven. Why?'

'I'm thinking you'd better turn in. Forget the rest of your watch. Doesn't matter much now, anyway, now that we know Butch is all right.'

Adrian thought about it, but couldn't look at Paul directly, didn't want to meet his eyes, because he knew what Paul was thinking. Then he peeled off his coat and headed for his sleeping bag. From there he whispered hoarsely and lamely, 'Don't *you* go!'

'I'm not that silly.'

Adrian grunted and unlaced his shoes and squirmed into the warm security of his blankets. It was so wonderful to lie down, to be safe, to be cosy, and to escape from himself. He closed his eyes tightly and clenched his jaws and sobbed to himself so that no one could hear. In three minutes he was asleep.

Paul still stood at the counter, wondering what he should do, really knowing what he should do, but every bit as aware of the dangers as Adrian had been. Wondering whether he should venture out, wondering whether the mist was as bad as Adrian said, even wondering whether Butch's sketchy account was reliable. Butch could have been imagining things. Adrian could have been imagining things. Adrian so often did.

Paul put on his shoes and the coat, took the rifle and the

lamp, glared at Adrian for a moment or two, and departed through the window.

He plodded up the street, feeling the bitter coldness of the air and the growing weight of his responsibilities. Adrian was too scared to do anything. Unless someone was beside him to hold his hand all his brave words meant nothing. Adrian was just a great balloon. Sometimes he was blowing himself up and other times he was flat. That's what he was. A balloon. All puffed up until someone let the air out or stuck a pin in him.

Paul came to the place where Adrian had lost his nerve, or near enough to it. This was where the mist seemed to be thicker, seemed to surround him and press upon him. Paul paused and listened carefully because Adrian had said he had heard the bull, but the stillness was so intense it throbbed in his ears.

He turned the lantern as high as he dared, and peered into the cold and wet little world that was about five yards square, because beyond it he could see nothing except the fog, tinted yellow by the flame of his lamp.

He was scared. Couldn't see far enough. Could so easily become lost. If Miss Godwin were out in this she'd be dead. It would kill her.

He couldn't go back. If he turned away he would be no better than Adrian. He would be a big balloon, like Adrian.

He climbed a few more yards, along the path that he used every schoolday of his life, and suddenly his hair almost stood on end.

He inhaled sharply, almost dropped the lamp, but it was Buzz, Buzz bounding out of the invisible world beyond the light.

Paul's nerves prickled up and down his spine and he panted, 'Golly, Buzz! Golly, boy, you nearly killed me with fright.'

Paul was very wary, tensed to dodge the snapping jaws of

the beastly little animal, but Buzz wagged his tail brightly. The dog was as friendly as it could have been.

'What's come over you?'

Paul deemed it wise to cement their friendship with a pat and he gingerly stroked the dog's head, and froze.

He didn't know why a sheet of paper on the ground should startle him so, but perhaps it was that he recognized it before he reached for it. It was a quarto sheet, typewritten, and it bore the number 206.

This was part of Miss Godwin's manuscript, part of her dearly loved book, blown from its rightful place on her cottage desk by the howling and heartless wind.

Paul felt suddenly desperate, suddenly frightened in a way he had never been frightened before. Homes might have crumbled, precious things might have been smashed, but this was something else. This sheet of paper was more than property; it was part of a person, almost a living thing.

He looked again, carefully, and saw two more sheets, one numbered 207 and the other 219.

Paul placed his rifle down and gathered them up gently and shivered in his sorrow for Miss Godwin. Not fully realizing why, he began to hunt for more, and in a few minutes had found thirty sheets of paper, all sodden, all muddied, and most of them unreadable.

Then he found something else, or perhaps it would be fairer to say that Buzz found something else, because Paul certainly would not have found it at that stage. Buzz's insistence was annoying because Paul had realized that he had mislaid the rifle, and he was anxious to get his hands on it again, but Buzz would not allow him. He barked and yelped and whined and did everything but talk.

Paul gave way and followed the dog only a short distance and came upon a heap of humanity, more muddied than any piece of paper, huddled at the foot of a tree, a woman, with a hundred or more rescued pages of her manuscript still clutched in her hand.

Paul's legs weakened and he found himself sitting beside her, too afraid to touch her, too nervous to reach out his hand to determine whether she was dead or alive.

CHAPTER TWELVE

In Possession

THERE was in the world an absolute stillness. That was how it seemed to Adrian. The earth had stopped revolving; moon, sun and stars had ceased to be; every living thing except himself had died. He was suspended in space, alone, and chilled to the marrow of his bones.

For a while his thoughts wandered in a wilderness, because everything seemed to be wrong. His bed was wrong; his body seemed to be bruised; and he couldn't break through to the reason for his confusion and anxiety.

Everything seemed to be damp and bitter and he wasn't breathing easily. Couldn't breathe properly at all. The air was like a poisonous gas.

He tried to sit up, but a pressure like a band of metal was bearing against his chest. He struggled against it and was suddenly wide awake and the mystery rolled back into the shadows of his mind.

Yes, he knew where he was. He knew that the town was dead and that a new day had come, and that the band across his chest was the constriction of the sleeping bag, and that the air wasn't poisonous, though it was certainly bitter, and that something truly was wrong.

It was daylight, yet it wasn't daylight. It felt very, very early in the morning, but he knew it wasn't. He knew he had slept, but he wasn't refreshed. It was a quarter to seven.

The light was strange and grey and unearthly. It wasn't an even light, but seemed to wander through the shop like a cloud, as though it were a cloud of pale light in a dark world.

There were no sounds from the birds, no barking dogs, no crowing fowls. Nor could he hear the beating of the diesel in the power shed, or voices, or cattle, or anyone splitting wood for the morning fire.

There never had been a day like this, never before in the history of Hills End. This wasn't an ordinary day. This was the day of desolation, of empty streets, and empty houses.

They were on their own. It was like waking up in a grave-yard and then wondering how one came to be there. One never really heard sounds until they were not there to hear. One never recognized them until they ceased. One never knew how friendly they were – all those families, all those sounds – until they had gone.

Adrian felt his courage withering. Could anything be worse than this? Was anything worse than a dead town?

He wriggled out of his sleeping bag and apparently the others still had not wakened. Even Butch was sleeping peace-fully, with an oddly dirty face. That shouldn't have been, be-cause Frances had cleaned his face with a damp towel. Adrian peered at him closely. Chocolate!

The last curtain in his mind was withdrawn. Of course there would be chocolate. There were the wrappers of two quarter-pound blocks near his pillow. And there was more, too – the inflooding of a deep depression, the memory of his failure on the hillside.

'Is that you, Paul?'

'No.'

Gussie emerged from her sleeping bag, groaning a little and puffy round the eyes. 'Morning! Thank Heavens!'

'Yes.'

'What an awful night! I don't think I slept a wink. I'm frozen stiff.'

She'd slept all right. Adrian knew that, and Frances was stirring and Maisie opened her eyes.

'Washing with that lemonade,' said Gussie, 'was a glum idea. My skin feels terrible.'

Adrian didn't hear her. He was on his feet looking for Paul, wondering where he had slept. Only two lamps were burning; the third, perhaps, had gone out, but where was it? And the trouble with the air in here was fog, a thick and nasty fog. It could not have been worse outside. It seemed as though the outside had come inside – as it had. The panel in the boarded-up window was down and the fog had drifted in, crept in, writhed in like something evil.

Adrian already sensed what had happened, but he didn't want to admit it, not even to himself, for many reasons.

'What's wrong, Adrian?'

He glanced down and Frances was looking at him.

'I don't know,' he said.

'Where's Paul?'

'He doesn't seem to be here, and there's a lamp missing.'

'What do you mean?' screeched Gussie. 'Paul not here! Why isn't Paul here?'

Adrian didn't know what to say, and they were all awake now, even Butch, and Butch seemed more refreshed than any of them. Butch was padded so well with fat that any bed was a soft bed. And no smell, even fog, worried him.

'Hi, everyone,' he said, 'Miss Godwin here yet?'

Adrian shook his head. 'How do you feel, Butch?'

'Goodo.'

'What's the chocolate doing all over your face?' said Frances quietly.

'Chocolate?' squeaked Harvey. 'Gee, I didn't get any chocolate.'

'No one had chocolate,' said Frances, 'except Butch. And why wasn't I wakened at three o'clock? Paul was going to wake me then. It was your watch, Adrian, until midnight; Paul's watch until three, and then mine until six. Something's gone wrong.'

'Don't be silly,' snapped Adrian. 'Of course nothing's gone wrong.'

'Where's Paul?' demanded Gussie.

Adrian groaned. 'How should I know? Maybe he's gone to bring the milk in.' The moment he said it Adrian could have bitten his tongue, because he saw that flicker of a memory in Butch's eyes, and heard Gussie's ironic laugh.

'Milk?' declared Gussie. 'What milk? There aren't any cows. Do we all look that silly?'

Butch, with a troubled frown, said, 'Who's silly? Adrian put the billy out. Last night he put it out. Who's silly?'

Maisie made her voice heard for the first time that morning, and she managed to hint at more than she said. 'No, Butch. Adrian's a bit of a loony, but he's not that vacant. He didn't put the billy out at all, did he?'

'Like I said,' stated Butch. 'He put the billy out. I saw him go. You even put your coat on, didn't you, Adrian?'

Adrian didn't know where to hide himself. It would have been so much wiser to have admitted the truth, but Adrian wasn't a very wise person. He blushed and mumbled, and Frances turned to Butch with kindness and firmness.

'You're mistaken, Butch.'

'Like I said.' Butch was showing his distress. 'Adrian put the billy out. Honest injun, I'm not lyin'. Tell 'em, Adrian!'

'Of course he's not lying,' snapped Gussie with her usual intuition. 'Adrian's hiding something. Adrian knows something about Paul that he doesn't want to tell us.'

Adrian flared. 'I don't know anything about Paul.'

'Well, what were you doing in bed?' Maisie demanded. 'You must know something because you had to wake Paul when you changed watch. Who was it that gave Butch the chocolate, anyway?'

Butch pointed and he was looking at Adrian with bewilderment and hurt. 'Adrian did – after I told him about Miss Godwin an' all. Don't you remember, Adrian? After that you went to put the billy out.'

Adrian knew he was silly to deny it, but he couldn't help himself. 'I don't know what you're talking about.'

Frances interrupted, 'Exactly what did you tell Adrian, Butch? Perhaps you dreamt it, you know.'

Butch was close to sobbing. 'It wasn't a dream, 'cos I didn't steal the chocolate. Adrian gave it to me. I told him about Miss Godwin most likely bein' up on the old log trail. Like I said, I thought we was together all the time. What are you all gettin' cross with me for? I haven't done nothin'. And then Adrian took the lamp and his coat *and put the billy out!*'

Adrian was cornered and the situation was out of hand. He had been shamed as he had never been shamed and he didn't know how to salvage his self-respect or restore Butch's broken trust in him. He couldn't look anyone in the eye, least of all Butch, and he knew now that his failure on the hillside, which could have remained a secret with Paul, was as good as being public property.

He heard Gussie screeching at him. 'You horrible beast, Adrian, what are you hiding from us?'

Adrian wanted to run away, but he didn't have the courage

to do that either. 'Paul's all right,' he mumbled. 'Paul's brave –'

'Where is Paul?' screeched Gussie.

'I don't know, but I suppose he's looking for Miss Godwin. He said he wouldn't go, but I guess he's gone.'

'When?' demanded Frances.

'I dunno. I dunno.'

'Why did Paul go,' accused Maisie, 'when it was you that Butch told?'

Suddenly Adrian shouted at them. 'Yes, I did go, and I told Butch I was putting the billy out. I tried, while all you lot were sound asleep, snoring your rotten heads off. I went up that mountain, in the fog, in the dark, by myself. I *did* try!'

He turned then, and ran. He stumbled along the counter and out through the hole in the window into the fog.

'Let him go,' said Frances quietly. 'I think we'd better leave him alone.'

Frances might have been calm on the outside, but Gussie was becoming hysterical.

'What's happened to Paul? How long has he been gone? He might be lost. He might be dead. We've got to go and look for him.'

'Please, Gussie,' appealed Frances. 'Paul knows how to look after himself.'

'You can see the fog' – Gussie's voice was quivering – 'you can see the window has been open for hours or the shop wouldn't be full of it. He's probably been up on that mountain nearly all night. He might be miles away, drowned, or anything.'

'You don't get drowned on a mountain,' grumbled Harvey. 'Girls are silly.'

'Yes, Gussie,' said Frances, 'do be sensible. He might have got up at daylight and gone then.'

'And taken a lamp with him? In daylight? You know as

well as I do he's been gone all night. It's Adrian's fault. I hate him.'

'It's my fault,' mumbled Butch. 'That's whose fault it is. If I hadn't lost Miss Godwin no one would have had to go and look for her at all. And now everyone's in trouble. Now we're all fightin' and arguin', all because of me.'

'Oh, Butch!' Gussie suddenly felt awful, because they all regarded Butch as a little boy, and not as a big boy. 'Oh, Butch, you know we don't mean that.'

'Adrian's my friend,' said Butch with a sniff. 'You don't mean it about Adrian, either, do you?'

Gussie sighed deeply, couldn't find the right words, so shook her head.

'Good,' said Frances, 'that's better. I think we can all learn a lot from Butch.' Frances seemed to pull herself together. 'This won't do at all. I must put the breakfast on. After we've had breakfast – well, the fog might have cleared by then, anyway.'

'I'll help you,' said Gussie.

'No, no, no. I – I'd rather have no one near me.'

'All right. We'll go outside and have a look round. Coming, Maisie?'

'All go outside,' said Frances. 'Please. All except Butch. He can open the tins for me.'

'I'm not goin' anywhere with those silly girls,' said Harvey. 'I haven't had me wash yet.'

'What?' shrieked Maisie. 'You wash? Since when?'

Harvey drew himself to his full height, which wasn't much, tossed his head haughtily as he had seen the film stars do, and stalked into the store-room.

'Goodness!' said Gussie. 'Perhaps we've misjudged him.'

'Boys are impossible.' Maisie sniffed. 'You don't know where you are with them. They're all the same. If they're not strutting like peacocks they're blubbing their eyes out.'

'Eh?' said Butch.

'That's what my mum says,' declared Maisie, 'and my mum knows. Coming, Gussie?'

Gussie shrugged. 'That's what I asked you.'

Butch stared after them and thought about Maisie, and looked at Frances. 'Is that true?' he asked.

Frances smiled and thrust the tin-opener into his hands. 'Baked beans, Butch.'

Outside, Maisie and Gussie took a few paces and halted. They couldn't see very far – the fog was like soup – and it did something to them, immediately subdued them, and Gussie couldn't carry her thoughts beyond Paul. 'The fog isn't good, Maisie. This fog is like the wet season. It's like the fog we get that lasts for days.'

Maisie found herself nodding.

'And that means,' said Gussie, 'that the aeroplane won't be able to find us again, and that no one will be able to come along the road, and that we won't be able to get out again, either?'

Maisie knew what Gussie was thinking and she said, 'I suppose so, unless our families are almost here now. It's two days. They must be nearly back.'

'I think something's happened or they would have been here long ago.'

'It can only be the bridge, Gussie. That'd stop them for a while. It would be terribly hard to cross the gorge without a bridge, 'specially with the river in flood.'

'Somehow,' said Gussie sadly, 'I don't think that'd stop my dad.'

Maisie looked away from her, because she couldn't lie, not even with her eyes. She knew, as Gussie knew, that it would need more than a broken bridge to stop their fathers.

'Paul's a chump,' Gussie burst out. 'Fancy going out into the dark with that bull still wandering round, and the fog, too.'

'Perhaps that's why he's not back, Gussie. Perhaps the fog caught him unawares.'

'Of course it did. Probably he's miles away, wandering in circles, or lying at the foot of a gully. Or even drowned in a gully. Oh, Maisie . . .' Gussie bit her lip and refused to cry. 'Paul does some awfully silly things. If we'd felt we could have helped Miss Godwin last night none of us would have gone to bed.'

'I don't think we can help her. I think she's dead.' Maisie turned away again. 'Come on, Gussie. Lets see what Frances is burning for breakfast.'

'I thought she told us to stay outside and have a look round.'

'What is there to look at? Perhaps the fog is a good thing after all. Who wants to look at things when they're broken?'

'You know,' said Gussie slowly, 'sometimes I've thought what fun it would be to be on our own, on a desert island, or something like that. No one to growl at you. No one to tell you what to do. No one to order you around. . . .'

She didn't say any more, but she bit so hard on her lip that she made it bleed and she grabbed Maisie's hand and almost dragged her back to the shop.

Frances was not concerned with the problems of the day ahead. Frances was concerned with her fear of this primus stove that seemed so determined to destroy everything she cooked, and for a while had even seemed determined to destroy her. The wretched old thing was worn out. It didn't burn with a clean blue flame as it should have done, but puffed out tongues of red fire and black smoke and stank to high heaven. She made up her mind that she'd never use it again. She'd take a new one down from the shelf and pay for it herself, rather than run this awful risk of setting light to the shop. The remotest chance that her actions could lead to a serious fire was enough to frighten the life out of Frances – as if she didn't have worries enough already, fretting for Paul's safety.

Frances felt this heavy responsibility towards everyone and everything. She even felt that she held the ruins of the town on trust, that she was personally responsible towards all the absent people of the town. She was half convinced that she was breaking the law merely by being in the shop and everything that was taken from the shelves was a pain on her conscience. She knew no one else looked at it in the same way, not even Paul, and that didn't help her. She carried the worry for them all, and when she discovered why that little beast Harvey had wanted to wash she could have choked him. He had the sink full of lemonade and was wallowing in it.

'Harvey!' she screamed.

Harvey jumped a foot, hiccuped violently, dodged the angry swing of Frances's hand, and ran for his life.

Frances sighed, pulled out the plug in the basin, and then called her charges for breakfast. 'You, too, Harvey. Come on!'

They all came, except Adrian, though Harvey took the precaution of grabbing his plate and retreating to the window end of the shop.

'Where's Adrian?' asked Butch.

'Call him, Harvey,' said Frances. 'He must be out there somewhere.'

There was no reply to Harvey's squeal, so they began their breakfast of baked beans, of sweet black tea made from the rain-water Frances had caught overnight in the bowls outside. The beans were soggy and the tea was like tar, and Frances couldn't understand why. Perhaps if there had been a few complaints she might have felt less upset about it, but all suffered in silence, even Harvey.

At last she couldn't stand it any longer – this stoic chewing and these grimly set young faces that continued to sip at her evil brew of tea, with Gussie even shuddering from head to foot. 'Why don't you say something?' she burst out. 'Why don't you tell me it's deadly?'

'It's all right,' said Maisie.

'It's not all right.' Frances suddenly swept her own tin plate from the counter and it clattered to the floor. 'It's awful, awful, awful!'

'I don't know about that,' said Gussie. 'Perhaps it's a bit gluey, but it's nothing to get upset about.'

'That's right,' said Butch. 'You should have seen the slop the boys cooked up when we went campin' last year. This is real high-class.'

Frances went out through the shop window into the open air, flaming with embarrassment, and Harvey scratched his head and squeaked, 'Talk about the ten little nigger boys! At this rate we won't have anyone left.'

Frances stumbled a few paces and stopped, trembling, regretting her flare of temper no less than her lack of cooking skill, but thankful for the moment to get away from everything. Of course the reasons went far deeper than a spoilt breakfast.

More and more were the fears for her family claiming her mind. That they had still failed to return, that another day had come to this dead town and that its silence seemed to be deepening hour by hour, were parts of these fears that were beginning to break her down. She had panicked once or twice yesterday, but that had been different. This was something else. This was like a sickness.

It wasn't fun being alone. It wasn't fun not knowing what had happened to the people she loved, her parents, her brothers and sisters, her friends, Paul, and even poor Adrian. Something had happened to Adrian all right. He seemed to be falling to pieces. It wasn't fun for Frances trying to be grown-up about everything when she was only thirteen years and three months old.

She wanted her mother. She wanted someone else to do the cooking and the worrying. It could have been fun, perhaps, being alone, in different circumstances. It could have been easier even this morning if the sun had blazed in, but the morning had crept in with this ugly, acid-smelling fog, this gloom, this dampness, this feeling of being the last people left on the earth. The morning had crept in as though it had not wanted to come at all, as though even the light of the morning had forgotten them.

The eighty-five miles to the town of Stanley ceased to be merely eighty-five. The distance began to roll away into a deep emptiness without measure or time. She could picture the town rushing away from her into space. She was cut off.

Then she saw a figure, indistinct and grey in the fog. She didn't stop to think. She immediately thought it was her father and rushed towards him.

'Daddy! Daddy!'

It wasn't her father. It was Paul, with the rifle and with haggard lines under his eyes, but with a smile so gentle that it astonished her. 'Sorry, Frances. Only me.'

'Oh, Paul. . . .' She pulled herself together and sought to cover up her embarrassment by snapping at Paul. 'Where on earth have you been? Hours and hours and hours. You've worried the lives out of us.'

Paul's expression changed suddenly to irritation. 'Oh, boil your head!'

He brushed past her and climbed over the sill into the shop and felt tired enough to lie down and die, but he heard Gussie's excited shout and was nearly knocked from his feet by the force of her rush.

'You're back,' Gussie cried, 'safe and sound. I thought you were dead. I thought you were dead.'

Paul groaned. 'Come off it. Dead? What are you talking

about. I've found Miss Godwin, that's all, but I'm too tired to carry her. Someone will have to help me.'

He leant against the counter and realized that he was responding to all their excitement and their chorus of praises. It came like an injection of new strength.

'Yes,' he said, 'she's alive, but she seems to have suffered an awful lot. She knows me, but I can't get any sense out of her. I suppose it was her book that did it.'

'What about her book?' said Gussie sharply.

'Blown all over the place. That's how I found her. She was looking for the bits, crawling all over the hill in the dark, picking up bits of paper. I suppose we've got about half of it.'

'We'll find the rest,' declared Gussie, 'even if it takes all day.'

'We've got to bring her back here first. She's been up there all night, on the school porch. Golly, it was a long night. . . . Has Buzz come back?'

'Buzz?' squeaked Harvey.

'That means he hasn't, I suppose. And what's wrong with Frances? Like a bear with a sore head. Practically threw her arms round me and then started abusing me.'

'Frances,' said Maisie wisely, 'has got the jitters.'

'Someone's got to help me find Buzz,' squealed Harvey.

'Buzz doesn't need finding. He'll find you when he's ready. Probably got his nose down a rabbit-hole.' Paul looked, then, from face to face. 'Butch, you'd better stop here. Keep an eye on things. The rest of you come with me and give a hand. . . . Where's Adrian? Yeah, where's Adrian?'

Maisie shrugged. 'Putting on an act, that's where he is. Caught out, that's what happened to Adrian. He's a great big puff of wind. Adrian doesn't fool me, like he fools some people.'

Paul glanced at Maisie warily. 'What are you talking about?'

They were surprised to hear Frances, surprised to see her standing at the window. 'You're being mean, Maisie. Adrian did his best – while *you* were asleep.'

Maisie glared but Frances silenced her. 'Are you people coming to get Miss Godwin, or not?'

'What about the bull?' squeaked Harvey.

'Really,' said Paul, 'what about it?'

Miss Elaine Godwin felt cold and frail and aged, but she was far more herself than Paul had known. She knew what the boy had done, just as she knew what the fat boy Christopher had done. Perhaps they had not saved her from death, but they had given her at least a few more hours of life.

She was humbled physically as she had never been humbled. Her proud independence didn't matter now because it had ceased to be. For years she had believed that she could go through life giving, without taking anything back. Even when the boys split wood for her stove she never allowed them to do it without payment. She was in no person's debt, man or woman or child. She was afraid of favours and sympathy. When the children had come to her two days ago on the hillside she had received them in dread. That she really needed sympathy and affection was obvious, or she would not have been afraid of it. Her pride did need to be broken. Her independence did need to be humbled. Until she learnt how to receive as well as to give she would never be wholly happy. But still she was broken in body, not in spirit. She was not really humbled at all.

Paul had left her, covered with his coat, lying against the wall of the school porch, but he had not been gone a minute before she was striving to reach the mud-stained sheets of paper which were her book, which the boy had weighted down unnecessarily with a stone.

It hurt her to sit up, but she refused to surrender to pain.

She wouldn't break. She wouldn't die with this remnant of her labour lying here to stir pity in the hearts of others. She'd never have them say, 'Poor woman. Isn't it pathetic? Surely she had done nothing to deserve it. Poor dear, of course she knew that insurance would rebuild her home, but nothing could rebuild her book.'

She thought back over the years. A dozen times she had sat down to type another copy of the manuscript, but every time something had stopped her. It all fitted together now into a pattern that could almost be called destiny. The book simply was not meant to be. Fame was not for her.

She stretched out and grasped the pile of sodden paper and squeezed until it became a mass of pulp, then she raised her pale eyes into the fog of the morning and saw that all the world beyond her was blotted out.

It was a symbol, and she was too bitter in her heart even to weep.

Butch's feet were sore and he didn't really know what to do with them. He hadn't said anything about it to the others because there seemed to be so many things that were more important. He hobbled here and there about the shop looking for relief, though he didn't know what he was looking for, not until he arrived in the store-room and saw the sausage machine.

Butch smiled his ready smile and sat on the stool near by and stared at the sausage machine and at the mincer and at the shelf above on which were arranged the ingredients used by Mr Matheson to make the sausages. It was gloomy, so he brought a lamp in from the shop and turned it up high and again sat on the stool and took it all in, in his thorough and laborious way.

It was a wonderful machine, the sausage machine. How was it that meat went in one end and sausages came out at the other? This wasn't a curiosity born of the moment, but a life-long fascination. Often Butch had stood at this door now behind him, and had watched the magical process in wonder. From as far back as he could remember he had admired those deft twists of Mr Matheson's wrists that transformed the slippery rope of meat-packed skin into neat little sausages. If, one day, Butch could mince the meat, mix it and blend it, and create from it a perfect string of perfect sausages he would know true bliss. If he could create sausages Butch would be happy, and if he could go on creating them he would be content to do so for the rest of his life.

He had mentioned it to Miss Godwin once and she had smiled at him. 'When you start making sausages, Christopher, be sure that they're the best you can make. Some men build bridges and some make sausages.'

Butch again went to the door, but the shop was still empty. He waited and waited, but no one came and he started trembling and still no one came.

He didn't really feel guilty, but he was shy. He didn't want anyone to catch him in case they made fun of him. It was because he was shy that he had never asked Mr Matheson to teach him how.

That was the trouble now. How did one begin?

He moved along the bench, inspecting the labels on the tins. There seemed to be so many of them. So many things to go in one little sausage – and then he found a sheet of paper stuck to the wall. It was a yellowed sheet of paper with many splash-marks over it and the ink that once had been bright and blue was dull.

His heart leapt because it was the recipe. It must have been the recipe for the sausages, because it didn't make sense for anything else. His excitement was so intense that it caught his breath.

Meat – 25 lb.
Wheatmeal – 4¼ lb.
Sugar – 6 oz.
Salt – 6 oz.
Seasoning – 2 oz.
Onion powder – ½ oz.
Preservative – ¾ fluid oz.
Water – 1 gal.

Butch shivered with emotion. This was real treasure. This was the recipe. He *knew* how to make sausages.

He smiled to himself. He had invaded the grown-up world and captured one of its secrets. Even his mother didn't know how to make sausages. Even his father didn't know. Frances didn't know. Paul didn't know. Adrian didn't know. Perhaps even Miss Godwin didn't know.

All he had to do now was make them and everyone would say how clever he was. He would work fast. He would do everything just as he had seen Mr Matheson do it, because he had known the motions even if he had not known the recipe. He would make the sausages and cook them and perhaps have them ready by the time the others were back.

He found the box of sausage skins beneath the bench, drew out one long length and shook the salt from it. He knew Mr Matheson always soaked the skins in water, so he took the bucket into which Frances had emptied all her precious water, poured half of it into the sink and kept the other half for the recipe.

Twenty-five pounds of meat! He opened the freezer door and was not repelled by the fearsome odour, because Butch had had an operation on his nose and had lost his sense of smell. How was he to know that the meat was decomposing and was loaded with poisonous organisms? The light was so bad he couldn't even see the colour of it.

CHAPTER THIRTEEN

Fog-Bound

AT 7.38 a.m., in the air-conditioned comfort of a broadcasting studio, more than a thousand miles from Hills End, far, far beyond the fog-shrouded slopes and the desolated forest, sat a pleasant young man. This was the young man whose duty it was to read the National News at 7.45.

Invariably this young man scanned his script beforehand. Oversea incidents had a habit of happening in places with unpronounceable names, and even though they were written in phonetics an unprepared reader could stumble and raise amused smiles in the homes of the educated – or, worse still, bring through the next morning's post a heap of letters from those crusty persons who forgave no errors of speech except the ones they committed themselves.

He rehearsed the tricky place names and thumbed back through the sheets to the main story of national interest, this rather grim story that was happening in the Stanley Ranges.

Floods were floods, destruction was destruction, but they were wounds that could heal. This was something different.

'Events in the flood-isolated north have taken a dramatic turn. Seven school-age children of Hills End and their mistress, Miss Elaine Godwin, are marooned or lost in remote mountain country, apparently beyond all hope of immediate aid. Repeated attempts to gain radio contact with the area have failed.

'The discovery late yesterday of seventy-two men, women and children trekking on foot through the bush twelve miles from Stanley solved the mystery of the missing population of Hills End. These persons had abandoned their motor vehicles after waiting, as they believed, in vain, for assistance from the outside world. The appalling conditions of the road that made so difficult their own escape from the mountains had delayed the rescue party, fifty strong, led by Police Constable Fleming.

'At the joining up of the two parties it was learnt that the failure of the brakes in the leading vehicle had prevented the picnic convoy from reaching Stanley before the onset of Saturday's cyclonic storm. All were safe and well, though cold and hungry, and reported that ten of their menfolk, with the balance of their food, had left the stranded convoy at daybreak to return on foot to Hills End, a distance back into the mountains from the convoy of approximately sixty miles. These ten men include the fathers of seven schoolchildren who had remained in Hills End to accompany their mistress on an expedition to what is known locally as "the Bluff". The Bluff, a high cliff riddled with caves, had been reported to contain a number of aboriginal rock paintings of great antiquity

'The plight of the children and their teacher is not known except that they should have been in the vicinity of Hills End early yesterday, but no sighting of any person, dead or alive, was made by the R.A.A.F. aircraft which closely surveyed the devastated area at midday.

'As reported in earlier bulletins, the airmen observed widespread destruction, landslides, extensive flooding, and a crazed bull, an accumulation of conditions which gives rise to the gravest concern. All bridges are cut and the main span of the bridge over the River Magnus Gorge, fifteen miles south of the township, was seen from the air to be wrecked. The collapse of this bridge, which won the Roger Morris Rural Developmental Prize for 1951, is a grievous loss to the district. It spanned the gorge at its narrowest point, bridging a gap of 147 feet, and it is not known at the present time how this formidable barrier, in conditions of flood, can be crossed from either direction.

'The ten Hills End men who are attempting to reach their town may know of an alternative crossing, but this is not considered likely. The little-known, but magnificent River Magnus, which is the northward-flowing arm of the Stanley River, cuts the ranges in two. The only other known approach, occasionally used by experienced bush-walkers, involves a wide re-routing through rugged country which, in favourable weather conditions, has been known to take five days and more. It is not conceivable that these ten men could be carrying food sufficient for more than two or three days. It is not possible at present to warn them that the bridge is down.

'It is reported this morning from Stanley that two parties of thirty volunteers, each including a doctor and each led by an experienced bush-walker, left at 3 a.m. to follow up the ten local men, one party taking the river road and the other the overland route. Low-lying cloud and continuing mist and rain are preventing the use of aircraft.'

Adrian was hungry, but too self-conscious, too ashamed, to return to the shop. Not really knowing why, except that he wanted to go home, he found himself climbing the terraced hillside upon which stood Hills End's most striking house. He found himself plodding round the wrecked house and opening the door from the back porch into the kitchen. Soon he was sitting at the table, with his feet in a puddle, beneath the gaping ceiling, chewing a damp cereal biscuit, and not enjoying it a bit, and trying to imagine that his parents were there with him.

What would his father do in a situation like this? Ben Fiddler was a resourceful man, a man of great faith in God. Why was it that he, Adrian, had inherited so little from him? Ben Fiddler was a man's man, but his son was feeble and silly in the head, an idle dreamer, a liar and a cheat, a coward, useless. Adrian was being hard on himself, but for the first time he believed he could see himself as others saw him. Adrian was wrong; his friends loved him, but he was too upset to remember it. He forgot all his own good points, and they were legion, and could remember nothing beyond the miserable figure he had made in the shop, lying, blushing, betraying his friends, trying to cover up his own cowardice.

It was all his fault. This terrible mess that everyone was in went right back to another of his stupid lies – the first lie he had told about the rock paintings, to divert his father's anger, when the truth itself would have been far, far better. He hadn't been to the caves at all that day, the day he had said he had found the rock paintings. Not to the caves. Nowhere near them. Not even out of his father's garage down at the roadside. How silly it was, because he had almost convinced himself that he had been to the caves. Instead, he had been fooling with his father's car and had broken a brake connexion, and it had taken all day, until dark, to repair it. An ingenious repair for a boy it was indeed, but Adrian didn't know that it had failed to see the distance to Stanley and that in the making of his repair he had rendered it impossible for anyone to repair it again.

What would his father do in this situation?

He wouldn't run away and sulk. He wouldn't look for excuses. When Ben Fiddler made a mistake he admitted it and got on with the job. He'd organize everything, as he always did, and give every man his particular task to do do. First of all he would reach for a sheet of paper and a pencil and write down everything that had to be done, and he would go over the list, again and again, to make sure that nothing was missed. Ben Fiddler had created a prosperous township in a wilderness when everyone had told him he was mad. Adrian's father had system. He didn't listen to the prophets of gloom. He had faith that everything would always turn out right in the end.

That Adrian began to think these things, and began to remember them, was proof enough that he had inherited some of his father's virtues. If the boy could put his finger on the things his father did right, he hadn't entirely failed his father, nor had his father failed him.

Adrian wandered into the ruined house until he came to his father's study, and he pushed the door open, and it took a lot of pushing because it had swollen. He could see the wreckage, he could feel the carpet squelching beneath his feet, he was aware of the fog that misted the outlines of the big room, but he came to the desk and sat in the wet chair. He wiped his sleeve across the surface of the desk, then took a notebook and a pencil from the drawer and started thinking hard.

The young folk found Miss Godwin leaning in a peculiar position against the inside wall of the school porch. She looked strange, because her eyes were open and seemed to be looking straight at them, yet without expression. She was propped almost upright, but she was limp and white. Beside her, near one fallen hand, was a shapeless mass of paper pulp. Her beautiful hair had come undone and hung in wet strands, like a blend of hemp and silk, so long that it spilled on the floor. They had never known her hair was so long and so fair and so beautiful.

'She's dead,' whispered Frances. 'Oh, my goodness, she's dead!'

Gussie's sob caught in her throat, but Paul, frightened as he was, lifted his teacher's cold and limp wrist, and felt frantically for her pulse.

'She's alive,' he blurted out, 'but she's far gone. She's terribly far gone.'

What was he to do? He should never have left her. Of course he had had to leave her. It was silly to comdemn himself. It wasn't his fault. It was one of those things.

'Give me your coats,' he said quickly. 'We've got to get some warmth into her and then we've got to get her back to the shop. She's got to have warmth, Frances. Hot-water bottles, a big fire. And a stretcher. What can we use for a stretcher?'

'Here,' said Frances, 'I'll wrap her up. You look for a stretcher.'

'But *what* can we use as a stretcher? I've had all night to think about it and it never crossed my mind.'

'Don't panic,' Maisie said calmly. 'If you can't find one, make one. Anyway, what's wrong with the classroom table? Turn it upside down.'

'Bless you, Maisie!'

Paul cracked the door open and recoiled in astonishment. He had spent so many hours huddled on the porch that he had forgotten the school was wrecked. He had expected to walk through the door into the classroom, but he stepped through the one remaining wall into a fog-shrouded ruin, a ghostly confusion of dangling roofing iron and broken timbers, of shattered window glass and of desks that had been crushed like cardboard beneath the tremendous weight of the trunk of the falling tree. Only the blackboard remained, and the platform from which Miss Godwin had taught a decade of children, and her chair, and her table.

He grabbed the table and jolted it over the edge of the platform, and found Harvey waiting to help him. Between them they manipulated it through the doorway and up-ended it on the porch.

He looked up then, straight into Gussie's face, and he knew something was amiss. Gussie's voice was horrified, shocked, and she presented to Paul a lump of paper pulp. 'Her book,' she breathed, 'she's destroyed her book . . . Paul, why would she do it?'

Paul felt suddenly sick and couldn't give an answer because there didn't seem to be one. He laid the paper down, almost reverently, within the rim of the upturned table, and said, 'Righto. Gussie and Maisie take her shoulders; Frances and Harvey her feet. I'll support her body. Be careful.'

They lifted her and placed her down and Paul said, 'Frances, we can manage here. Rush back to the shop and fix a bed for her. Heat some water and fill every hot-water bottle you can put your hands on. Mr Matheson's got a rackful of them. All right?'

Frances nodded and disappeared into the fog, and the children shuffled round the table, each took a corner, staggered to their feet, and slowly, carefully, nervously committed themselves to the mud and the hazards of the steep hillside.

Butch had minced his meat and blended his ingredients and even emptied his gallon of water into the tub and kneaded it, worked it through with his hands and arms until it was all mixed up, and sticky, and like a tub full of mud. He was a little dismayed by the quantity; there seemed to be so much of it; it would make so many, many sausages. There would be enough sausages to feed a multitude.

He threw his mixture into the machine, a big handful at a time, because that was the way he had seen Mr Matheson do it, but Mr Matheson didn't seem to get into the same sort of mess. It was mystifying. Butch had sausage meat everywhere, and with his first two throws towards the empty cylinder of the machine missed completely, and spread two great splotches along the bench and over the wall.

Butch scratched his head, because he knew that this was the way to do it. Mr Matheson didn't pack it in, he threw it in. What the reason was Butch didn't know, but everything had to be done the right way, so he picked up his third handful and threw again. It slapped into the cylinder with a lovely smack and soon he was throwing it heartily, chuckling to himself.

He had sausage meat on the floor and all round the sink and splashed over the window. He had it in his hair and ears and even in his pockets. He couldn't stand up straight for it. He slipped often, and once sat splosh in the middle of the tub. For several seconds, he remained stuck, puzzled, but happy. He couldn't remember when he had been happier. He heaved himself to his feet and sighed. Perhaps it was for the best, because when he looked into the tub it was all but empty. He had got rid of the meat he hadn't needed. It had been squirted to the four corners of the room.

He rubbed the meat from his clothes with a rag and scraped enough floor space clear to proceed with the real excitement. He pushed the plunger into the end of the cylinder, checked to see that the worm gear was engaged, and placed the handle over the end of the spindle and gave it two or three turns. He heard a gurgling, squelching sound and trembled all over. Three more turns and the first colour of meat appeared at the nozzle on the opposite end of the machine.

Butch squealed with delight and grabbed the length of sausage skin from the sink and trailed it across the floor while he fumbled to find the end. It really was a long piece of skin. There were yards of it and when he did find the end it seemed too small for the nozzle.

He worked it between his fingers and tried to push it into position. It wouldn't fit. It wouldn't go. He realized slowly that there must have been a special way. He wrestled with it, refusing to give up, until he was in an awful tangle and an ache of despair had killed most of his joy.

He was so bewildered by this baffling mystery that he didn't hear Frances until she screamed, 'Butch, Butch, Butch! Come away from that filthy stuff.'

His heart almost stopped and he stammered in confusion.

Yes, it was Frances, the last person on earth to be unkind, and she looked so angry. She was white with anger. She was shaking with it and she was still screaming at him, 'Come away, Butch; What's wrong with you, you stupid boy? Do you want to die?'

A joke was a joke – oh, yes, but this wasn't a joke. Frances wasn't even making fun of him, and he was used to that sort of thing. The little kids always made fun of him.

Butch blinked back his tears and was so confused, couldn't understand, couldn't make any sense out of the things that Frances was yelling. This on top of his disappointment was too much for him. Suddenly, the tears couldn't be held back and he sobbed, 'I want me mum. Me mum's always so nice to me.'

Frances still felt she couldn't step into that filthy room. 'Butch,' she cried, 'I'm not cross with you. I'm not angry. Don't you know the meat's bad? Can't you smell it?'

He raised his eyes and looked around the room and towards the open door of the freezer, over all that dreadful mess. 'Bad meat? Bad?'

'Oh, Butch, of course you can't smell it, you poor dear. You didn't know, did you?'

He shook his head. 'Bad?'

'You've got to get out of there. You've got to change your clothes. You've got to wash yourself with disinfectant. You'll have to have a bath in it, and gargle your throat. Oh goodness, Butch! You haven't put any in your mouth?'

'Raw meat?' Butch was shocked. 'I wouldn't eat raw meat. I'm not dirty.'

'Well, please, Butch, come on out. Let's shut the door.'

He obeyed and she slammed the door and shuddered and hastened behind the counter, grabbing soap and disinfectant and a towel. She slapped them down and said, 'Take these and run. Find yourself a nice puddle and have a bath. When you come back I'll have some clothes for you. And for Heaven's sake don't touch anything before you get out of the shop. Don't touch a thing.'

He took the articles and looked at her sadly. 'I'm sorry, Frances.'

'You didn't know.'

'And they would have been such beautiful sausages. I only had to work out how to put the skins on them.'

'All right, Butch. Please go.'

He went and she stood for a few moments, almost stunned, knowing that there were important things to do, but first took another bottle of disinfectant from the shelf and trickled it on the floor about the store-room door, then opened the door and emptied the rest of it inside, hoping it would be powerful enough to take the smell away.

She leant against the wall, breathless. Really, really, these perfectly impossible boys! Harvey in the lemonade, Butch in the meat, Adrian in a tantrum, and Paul – Paul on the hillside all night.

She had so much to do. She had to get a stove going, and a heater working. She had to boil water, make a bed, prepare a hot drink. Hurry. She had to hurry. Oh dear, how wonderful it would be if her mother could do all these things for her! Would her mother be able to cope, or would she be more helpless than Frances?

She bustled round the shop, talking to herself, refilling the primus stove with kerosene, igniting the spirits, deciding to prepare a cup of beef extract for Miss Godwin, reminding herself that the water for the rubber bottles must not be boiling, yet conscious all the time that something was missing.

She took the big kettle and reached for the water. It was the water that was missing.

The stretcher party reached the road and there they flopped down, breathless and aching, even hot. From Paul's brow sweat was streaming. He had carried only one corner of the table, but he had managed to take more than a quarter of the weight. If Adrian had been here it would have been so much easier, but Adrian, as usual, seemed to have dodged the hard work.

'I'm whacked,' gasped Gussie. 'Goodness me, how on earth have we managed to get this far?'

'Rest a while,' panted Paul. 'It'll be easier along the road.'

'I've barked my shin,' complained Harvey. 'You bloomin' girls ought to be more careful. You let it slip twice and I copped it both times.'

'We've all barked our shins,' said Paul, 'so pipe down.'

How was Miss Godwin? They didn't know. She hadn't moved except when they had jolted her, or slipped, or stumbled. They had done very well, those children, to negotiate the slope without an accident, and each one had struggled on past his or her normal strength, even Harvey.

They rested, breathing deeply, constantly aware of the pale face of their teacher, dreading the thought of lifting the table and battling on again, aware too, of desolation and solitude.

That each one was jumpy was obvious to the others, and Gussie was thinking about her desert island again, thinking what a stupid idea it had been, thinking of the stories she had read in which children had rejoiced to be alone for days on end, thinking of all the things she had imagined that one could do without grown-ups hanging round to spoil the fun. It didn't work out that way. This was a continual fight. She had never imagined that one would have to be brave. She had thought it would be nothing but fun.

One didn't realize how wonderful parents were, even though they were crabby at times, until they weren't there.

Perhaps they all sensed that something was wrong. Suddenly they were looking at each other, from face to face, nervously alert.

'Is it a snake?' whispered Harvey.

They ignored him.

'I heard it hiss. It's a snake.'

'Be quiet!'

Gussie felt an icy shiver. It wasn't a snake. It hadn't hissed. The sound came from the feet of a heavy animal stepping through mud.

'The bull!'

'Sshhh!'

They couldn't see it, but it was there, somewhere, and Paul wanted the earth to open up and swallow him. That was how he had felt the night before. He wanted it to open up and swallow Miss Godwin, swallow them all from sight. He didn't even have the rifle. Twenty minutes he had spent, at daylight, hunting for the thing and then he had taken it to the shop and left it there. He was defenceless, and worse; he was burdened with Miss Godwin and two girls and Harvey. Worse than defenceless, because he couldn't even run. None of them could run, because lying within the rim of the table was Miss Godwin.

'Where is it?' hissed Gussie.

'Don't move. Don't breathe . . .'

It was there. Paul could see it, a misted form taking shape in the fog, squelching along the road.

'Freeze,' whispered Paul.

It was the bull all right, mooching along the road, from the open end of the town towards the shop. It wasn't wild, it merely looked pathetic.

They froze, as Paul had said, not moving, scarcely breathing. They couldn't have done anything else, anyway. They were too terrified to have run. Harvey's face turned a dirty grey and he closed his eyes and couldn't look.

Paul moved his eyes, but nothing else. He seemed to turn to stone except for his eyes, and the bull came on, plod, plod, squelch, squelch, past them.

Maisie groaned faintly, and started trembling violently in every limb and joint, and the harder she tried to stop it the worse it became.

Paul could have screamed at her, but didn't dare open his mouth, didn't dare move but he cast a glare on her that should have withered her up.

She couldn't stop it.

The bull moved on into the fog, lost its solidity, became a shadow, and was gone.

Gussie collapsed in a heap, panting for breath, and Maisie whispered, 'I'm sorry, I'm sorry, I'm sorry.'

'Quiet,' Paul whispered fiercely.

They waited, while Harvey's eyelids gradually parted and his eyes became larger and larger until Paul feared they were about to pop out of his head. They waited until the last sound had gone, until they could hear nothing but the throbbing silence and the strange and subdued rumble that was the river.

Paul sighed. 'Righto. Relax . . .'

'Oh dear!' groaned Gussie.

Paul's throat was dry and his tongue seemed to have swollen. Perhaps it had. Nothing in the world could surprise him now.

'Come on,' he said. 'Let's go.'

'*That* way?' whined Maisie. 'The bull went that way.'

Paul didn't like the idea either, but he said, 'We can't stop here, and we can't go any other way. Can we?'

There was no answer to that except a brief shake from three frightened young heads.

They heaved the table up and set off, following the path of the bull. They had shuffled no more than twenty or thirty yards when a terrified scream almost started them out of their wits. They actually dropped the table with fright. It was Frances.

Frances's problem was the water that Butch had so thoughtlessly used. Butch didn't understand that water was valuable. It was water to him whether it flowed in a river, lay in a ditch, or was conveniently located in a bucket. Butch didn't fully understand that flood waters stirred up the debris of years and were not safe to drink. They were usually safe enough to wash in, and the pool that Butch found for himself in the road was comparatively harmless even before he dutifully emptied into it his bottle of disinfectant. Thereafter any germs that survived deserved to survive.

Butch was always thorough and he stripped to his briefs and had a really good scrub, despite the bitter cold of the water. He didn't go near his clothes again. He left them yards from the pool, and it was a shame because they were the nice new clothes that had replaced his own ruined ones. He truly had made a mess of them. What on earth had possessed him? He must have gone silly for a while.

Butch was impressed enough by Frances's words to realize that the mud he stirred up in the pool didn't matter. Even if he transferred the mud to his body, as he did, it didn't matter, so long as he shifted the last remnant of his sausages. Butch was much more distressed by what he had done than Frances realized. Butch, deep inside, was a clean person. He might have seemed a little grubby to some people, but it was usually wholesome dirt. Butch could never eat food that anyone else had touched, could never share a sandwich or a piece of fruit. He had seen little children pick up apple cores and he had always snatched them away, and more than once had been scolded for it because others had believed he was stealing from babies. That he had actually handled bad meat offended him dreadfully, so much so that he still forgot the condition of his feet until he began to dry himself. They started hurting again, and that brought his thoughts sharply into the focus of his surroundings.

He looked up, still with the mud-stained towel in his hand, and there was Rickard's bull regarding him angrily, swaying its big head, snorting into the cold air two distinct puffs of vapour. It looked like the devil, complete with horns.

He started backing away from it, in horror, and had retreated only a few yards when he tumbled over a length of timber and fell heavily into wreckage of the hall. He let out a tiny cry and realized he was trapped. The wreckage was all around him except in the direction from which the bull was coming.

Frances had taken another bucket and had ventured into the fog to find clean water. She knew there shouldn't be any real difficulty because pure rain-water would lie in the hollows of buckled sheets of iron or even in storage tanks that had fallen but had not completely shattered. That anything would have done for the hot-water bottles did not for the moment occur to her. She was really too cross with Butch to think straight. Rather than have to plan for herself she desperately needed someone else to direct her, to tell her what to do. First and foremost Frances was a sturdy work-horse, not a leader.

The nearest wreckage was the hall, and it was amongst its tangle that Frances dragged her bucket, bailing water from where she found it a cupful at a time. It was slow work, because she was so impatient and so overwrought, and when she snagged the hem of her dress on a nail her annoyance was far out of proportion to the damage she had done. With very little trouble she could have freed the dress without harm, but she tugged on it irritably and ripped it.

The shock of what she had done pulled her up, made her try to steady down, but it wasn't as easy as that. Two days of privation and anxiety couldn't be dismissed in an instant. If a night's sleep couldn't cure it, a few seconds' pause couldn't touch it. The tensions had been building up, straining her nerves tighter and tighter, expanding towards breaking point. It was in that moment of conflict that she heard a faint cry, and she was so nervously alert that she knew its direction by instinct and her eyes were as quick as her ears. She actually saw Butch fall. She knew it was Butch because there was no one else in town so pink and so plump and so much the size of a man, and beyond, misted and vague, loomed the bull.

Frances broke. She gulped all the air it was possible for her lungs to contain and released it with a scream that expressed all her loneliness and all her helplessness and all her fear. She dropped the bucket with a clatter and lost the water on the ground. She ran away, because she couldn't bear to see Butch killed.

CHAPTER FOURTEEN

Adrian Fights Back

BUTCH could see death staring at him. Life had its problems for a fat boy of slow wits, but it had held no problem as big as this. Butch wanted to live more than anything else in the world. He never went looking for trouble as some people looked for it, but he wasn't a coward. Perhaps he was fighting to save only his own life, but he wouldn't die with his eyes closed. He heard the shriek from Frances, he had never heard anything like it, and that might have been the shock that moved him to face his peril.

The bull was pawing the ground and snorting and was as wild as a rhino, but Butch leapt from the debris into which he had fallen, wrenching free a length of jagged timber that normally he would have hesitated to handle. There were nails in it and it was splintered at one end to the sharpness of a spear, and it was fully eight feet long, four inches by two. It was a stud from the broken wall and a fearsome weapon, if he had the strength to use it.

Butch did have the strength and he never even wondered where it came from. He faced the bull, legs braced, fiercely glaring, breathing through open lips and clenched teeth, rapidly taking the feel of the piece of wood until it balanced above his right shoulder.

'Please, Jesus,' he hissed. 'I'm a good boy.'

He saw the bull coming, but didn't hear it. He heard nothing, not even his own shrill cry. He saw the beast so close that the beads of mist on its massive neck were glistening like jewels, and he heaved. He flung his piece of timber with all his might and with all the ferocity of his belief that Jesus wouldn't let him down, and immediately leapt to his right.

He landed on his knees, and heard the frightful crash as the bull ploughed, bellowing, into the wreckage of the hall. It was on its knees as he was, with the point of the spear embedded in its shoulders, but with six or seven feet of the shaft snapped off. More than that, it was fighting to free itself in its terrible rage, smashing timbers and plaster like eggshell.

Butch picked himself up to escape and Paul floundered into his vision, running like a madman. Paul was reeling, but he dragged Butch across the street towards the shop, groaning to frame his words, 'Where's Frances, Frances, Frances?'

'I dunno. Did anything happen to Frances?'

'She screamed. Surely you heard?'

Butch shrugged. 'Wasn't the bull. He was after me, not her. But I got him. I got him instead.'

Paul halted beside the shop, panting, 'How do you mean – you got him?'

'I speared him.'

Paul didn't argue, didn't exclaim his surprise, because it was true. He could see it was true in Butch's earnestness, and he could hear that it was true in the frightful sounds from the tormented bull.

'Between the shoulders.' Butch smiled. 'Like a matador.'

'You stood up to that animal – alone?'

'Not alone,' said Butch simply, 'but with Jesus, like Mr Fiddler says.'

Paul was awed, because the bull, it seemed, had even ripped the clothes from Butch, even torn him with its horns. A great red weal, a foot long, was scorched across his back.

What could Paul say? He didn't really understand it any more than Butch did.

'I'll get the rifle,' he mumbled, 'and finish the brute off.'

Paul scrambled through the window, more dazed than purposeful, and saw the rifle lying on the counter, and suddenly saw something else beyond, that struck despair into his heart.

Fire was licking the wall of the shop and the old primus stove was issuing clouds of black smoke and flaring with an ugly flame three or four feet high. It had ignited a display card hanging overhead and spread to the top shelf. Glory be, the shop was on fire.

He screamed at the top of his voice, 'Fire! Fire! Fire!' and snatched from the floor two of the bags they had laid over the spilt honey, then hesitated, momentarily lost, overcome by the accumulation of troubles and frights and dangers.

Butch tumbled through the window opening behind him and provided Paul with the spur that he needed. He raced along the counter, suddenly aware of the serious risk of explosion. There were bottles of methylated spirits and turpentine, tins of kerosene and paints. There was enough stuff near the fire to blow the shop sky-high. He slapped both bags over the stove and tried to smother it and yelled for the fire-extinguisher. Butch didn't know where it was and neither did Paul, and the bags failed to smother the stove.

'More bags,' screamed Paul. 'Call the others. We need help.'

And Paul started dithering, started panicking, and Butch was running in circles, not really knowing what he was looking for.

'Bags, Butch! Bags!'

Butch grabbed them from the floor and floundered towards Paul, but by the time he got there Paul had changed his mind again and had decided to throw the stove outside. He held it at arm's length and ran to the window, trailing a frightening cloud of inflammable vapour through which the hungry fire leapt and cracked. He pitched it through the window as far as he could throw it, and it had scarcely left his hands before he saw the injured bull weaving through the fog, bellowing, tossing its head and writhing its shoulders in pain. It had smashed through the wreckage of the hall and from one horn even trailed a bedraggled curtain.

The stove flamed out through the mist and exploded against the ground, not so much with sound, but with a sheet of yellow fire, and the bull stampeded in its final panic. It rushed into invisibility towards the hills, back towards its home.

Paul swung on his heels, panting, shaking, with a sharp pain in his side that came as much from fear as from breathlessness. Butch was frantically beating at the flames with a bag, but seemed to be feeding the fire with the draught. He wasn't getting anywhere, and the fire had to be stopped or the shop was gone.

'Stop it, Butch!' he screamed. 'You're making it worse.'

Paul spun along the counter, desperate for help. He wanted water, but there wasn't any; he wanted an extinguisher but couldn't find it; at least a few buckets of sand, but not even any sand.

'Stop it, Butch!'

Paul dragged the fat boy from the counter and panted, 'No, no, no! Some other way.'

Frances appeared at the window, deathly white, took one look and sobbed in bitter dismay. She didn't see Butch, didn't see Paul, saw only the fire crackling up the wall into the rafters.

Surely it couldn't be happening? Surely they had taken enough without this, too? It was her doing. In her haste she had used that beastly old stove again when she had vowed that she wouldn't.

She threw herself over the window-sill and saw the boys, standing helplessly, actually watching it burn, doing nothing, gaping. That one was Butch and that he was alive didn't register, but that the other was Paul did register, and she shrieked, 'Do something! Put it out!'

Paul scarcely seemed to hear her. He seemed to be mesmerized, as he was, by his own helplessness, and by the simple fact that too much had happened. He had reached his peak and passed it. Frances felt she wanted to hit him, but she rushed past him to the store-room door, flung it open, and slithered into that awful room. The extinguisher was beside the sink. She dragged it from the wall and smashed the glass seal on the edge of the bench and skidded out of the room again, turning on the tap, and directing before her an intense spray of liquid.

Paul saw her coming and had sense enough to dodge the vapour and thrust Butch out of its path. He stepped in beside Frances and took the extinguisher from her and vaulted on to the counter top and had smothered every flame in less than twenty seconds. The wall and the rafters were charred and smoking, but the fire was out.

He remained standing on the counter, sheepishly, fumbling for the tap to turn the extinguisher off.

'We couldn't find it,' he said. 'Didn't think of the store-room.'

Frances nodded and wanted very badly to cry, but she didn't. She had become aware that it was Butch who was beside her, absently licking honey from his fingers. She didn't understand why and was much too near hysteria to question anyone. Instead, she said, 'It was my fault, anyway. I shouldn't have left the stove unattended. . . . I'll light a new one.'

Her hands were trembling so violently that Paul said, 'I'll light it for you.'

'No, no. You – you get Miss Godwin. Butch, find yourself some clothes, or you'll catch your death, then get me some water. You used it in your filthy old sausages so you can get it for me.'

Paul didn't know what she was talking about, but Butch did, and all went their separate ways.

Adrian came down into the township with a slender notebook in his pocket and a very fat volume tucked under his arm. He was escorted by a pack of dogs – a boxer, two spaniels, a collie, a Scottie, and the infamous mongrel terrier known to his master as Buzz. Where they came from Adrian didn't know, except that their sudden appearance had given him a big fright.

They were the dirtiest looking dogs he had ever seen, caked in mud, but in boisterous good humour, obviously delighted to find him and all too affectionate. They jumped over him and pawed him, barking and yelping with excitement, and he wisely decided that there were too many of them to resist. Adrian had to take their mud and suffer it. He didn't want to be torn to pieces. Dogs in a pack were not to be argued with.

Adrian had reached a decision, and it was a difficult decision for a boy so burdened with his fears of what other people thought of him. Adrian liked to be on top, and usually was, where there was no real challenge to his courage. That by his own actions he had dropped to the bottom had forced him to look hard at himself, and his judgement was much harder than the judgement of his friends. They understood him better than he understood himself.

He had admitted that he was a coward. He had admitted that Paul had gone out in the middle of the night to carry on with a job that he had started. He had eaten his humble pie and all he really wanted to do now was hide. But he couldn't hide. He had to return to them and face them, but it was not his nature to return to the bottom. He had to go back and climb to the top again. He admitted to himself that he couldn't sit on top if it were to demand physical bravery. He wasn't made of the right stuff, but if he set his mind to it he could think and he could plan. And he had done that. He had planned for more than an hour at his father's desk, picturing Hills End as it had been and as it was now, gradually seeing it not as a wreck but as a tremendous challenge.

Gradually, Adrian had become excited. With no one to hear him and no one to see him, working only in his own mind, carried forward by the power of his imagination, lost in his concentration, he had devised his plan as his father had done, years before him. His only doubts had come when he had finished, when he had started down the hill. How was he to convince the others? How was he to regain their confidence? They'd laugh him out of the shop. Some boys could laugh themselves out of those situations by laughing with the people who laughed at them, but not Adrian. If they laughed at him it would be the finish.

In the midst of the yapping dogs he moved towards the shop, still excited, but nervous, still blushing whenever he thought of the miserable spectacle he had made of himself before his friends. That had been early in the morning, about seven o'clock, but now it was well after nine and the fog had lost its density. Perhaps the warmth of the invisible sun was managing to penetrate deeper into the great cloud bank.

Perhaps the clouds were lifting. Perhaps soon the fog would begin to swirl up out of the valley and vanish into nothing, mysteriously, as it sometimes did.

How wonderful it would be to see the sun again!

Yes, the fog was going up, because he could see the timber mill and the river of mud that was the Magnus, still high above its banks, but less violent, less far-reaching than it had been. He could see the power shed, still standing in the midst of destruction. Its floor was of concrete eight inches thick, and its walls and roof were of iron, bolted together. It was strong enough to survive almost anything.

And there was the shop, visible now, at a hundred and fifty yards. Deserted it seemed to be. The sound of the dogs had brought no one out. Perhaps they were not there!

Could it be that he was alone? Could it be that they had fled or journeyed out towards the bridge at Fiddler's Crossing? No, they would have gone to search for Miss Godwin! Or perhaps Paul had not returned. His thoughts and emotions were possessed by one doubt after another, and he realized he had caught himself at his old game. He was allowing his imagination to run away. He was frightening himself simply by thinking of things that might not have happened. His plan would never work if fear were permitted to tangle him up again.

He moved off, went a few more yards, then saw a movement at the shop window. He could have sworn it was the barrel of a rifle. That really startled him until he heard Paul calling, 'Come on! I thought you might have been the bull.'

Adrian hurried on with all the speed he could produce, short of breaking into a run. He had forgotten the bull, not entirely, but certainly as a threat to himself. The dogs accompanied him joyfully and he became aware of them again. With six dogs to protect him, no bull could hurt him, so he slackened his pace to

a carefree amble and arrived at the shop window feeling pretty
sure of himself.

Three heads were there to greet him – Paul, Maisie and
Harvey. Harvey, certain that he had recognized Buzz's bark,
was overjoyed and leapt to the ground and romped with his
dog. Maisie, too, had heard her family's boxer, and hugged
the bedraggled thoroughbred to her, and for an instant thought
again of the twenty-five guineas he had cost, but if he had cost
a hundred pence or a hundred pounds it wouldn't have made
any difference.

Maisie, then, glanced towards Adrian. 'Thanks for finding
him,' she said. 'I – I just didn't guess that you'd gone looking
for the dogs. I've thought some awful things about you. I'm
sorry. . . .'

Adrian knew he had gone pale and he saw Maisie's words as
yet another test of his honesty. Maisie didn't mean them that
way, but Adrian knew if he dared let them pass unanswered
his self-respect would be gone again.

'I didn't find the dogs,' he said. 'They found me.'

Perhaps Maisie didn't hear him, or if she did she was kind
enough to ignore it. 'Thanks,' she said. 'I'm so glad you've
brought him back.'

'Where have you been?' said Paul.

'Home.'

Adrian climbed over the sill and dropped inside. 'Did you
get Miss Godwin?'

Paul nodded coolly. 'Didn't think you cared, but we got her.
And we got a lot more. We've had trouble one way and another. I hope you were comfortable at home?'

Adrian started trembling. They were going to abuse him.
Before long they'd be laughing and jeering. He took a deep
breath.

'How is Miss Godwin?'

'Why don't you take a look for yourself?'

Adrian brushed past Paul and saw Gussie and Frances regarding him from the distance, without expression, and saw Butch with his usual, generous, cheerful smile.

'Hi, Butch,' he said.

'Hi, Adrian.'

Adrian's nostrils started twitching to a nasty odour. The smell in the gloomy shop was most unusual, like a doctor's surgery, like something burnt and smouldering, like something bad. There had been trouble, all right, as Paul had said.

'Adrian has been home,' Paul said loudly, 'to have a rest. To get away from it all. Lucky Adrian.'

It was an awkward silence, and Adrian didn't quite know what to do with it. He felt, deep inside, that it wasn't right that he should break that silence, because he'd be bound to try to defend himself. The trouble was he didn't know whether the others agreed with Paul or disagreed with him. He didn't know whether they were sympathetic or hostile. Then he saw Miss Godwin, lying like a dead person, wrapped up in blankets, with a kerosene radiator beaming its heat on to her, and he forgot his own problem and walked to her quietly and looked down into her white face.

Her eyes were closed, but she was breathing.

Adrian grunted to himself, heavily, and felt like a Judas, and saw then, beyond Miss Godwin, dozens and dozens of pieces of paper on the floor, wrinkled and torn, that had been peeled, like the skins of an onion, from a screwed-up lump of paper pulp. Instantly, he knew what it was.

Adrian was always a sensitive person; it was his nature. He could feel things. And he could feel something at this moment. It was like a black cloud pressing down upon everyone. He had the strangest feeling that they had given up, that they were all beaten. Just what had happened he didn't know. Yes, and there had been something in Maisie's manner – Maisie, of all his friends usually the most matter-of-fact – that hadn't been healthy, an unusual tremor in her voice, a nervousness about her, as though she had been trying to fight down a desire to scream.

Adrian sighed and caught a glimpse of the charred wall, of Frances, of Gussie, of Butch smiling no longer, and heard the footsteps behind him that were Paul's.

Adrian closed his hand tightly on the notebook in his pocket, placed on the counter the fat volume he had carried beneath his arm, and turned to face Paul again. 'Leaving me out of it, what's wrong?'

Paul wasn't as full of nastiness as Adrian had thought. His lip trembled. 'Everything.'

'In what way?'

'You were telling us yesterday – golly, was it only yesterday? – you were telling us that you heard my dad and your dad talking...' Paul looked very young. 'They said if we were left on our own to fend for ourselves we'd die. Honest, when I thought about it afterwards I reckoned they were silly. Of course we wouldn't die . . .' Paul paused again, perhaps frightened, perhaps embarrassed, perhaps doubting the wisdom of what he was about to say. He looked at his feet. 'We've only been alone two days and – and –'

'And look at us now?' suggested Adrian.

'Yeah.'

'But it's the third day, really, isn't it?'

Paul shrugged. 'What's the difference? We *can't* take it. We can't survive. Every single one of us, one after the other . . . Surviving is so much more than just finding something to eat. We haven't even got a leader. There's not one of us strong enough . . . That's why we're not captains at school. We're all right while someone else is telling us what to do. We're just not getting anywhere. We're all arguing and squabbling and being nasty.'

Paul started shaking and finally burst out with his greatest woe, '*And what are we going to do with Miss Godwin?*' He couldn't stop his tears then and it was a long, long time since he had cried with anyone watching. 'Even she wasn't strong enough,' he choked. 'Even Miss Godwin. She tried to destroy her book.'

How odd it was! Adrian could see that Paul wasn't the only one. Paul, perhaps, had been up all night and was exhausted, but the others were not exhausted. Yet they were just as low in spirits. Adrian had to be fair, he had been like it himself, but he wasn't now. He could feel himself growing stronger, he could feel his hand closing even more tightly about his notebook; he could almost feel himself turning into a man like his father.

'Perhaps you'd better tell me what's happened,' he said. 'I know if I'd been here I wouldn't have been much help, but please tell me.'

'You don't care. As long as you're all right, you don't care. Frances tells me you've been away for nearly three hours.'

'Two and a half.'

'You ran away like a little boy who couldn't have a lollipop.'

Adrian, suddenly, was treading on thin ice again, was getting nervous again, because Paul was being nasty again, but Frances said, in a very quiet and humble voice, 'Adrian wasn't the only one, was he, Paul? Was he, Maisie? Was he, Gussie?'

So Frances told him what had happened, in a halting voice and then said with her first tone of accusation, 'Are you sure you didn't know any of it? Are you sure you didn't hear?'

'I was in the house,' said Adrian, 'there's a thick fog, I'd shut the doors. I didn't hear because I was thinking.'

'Thinking?' exploded Paul.

Adrian took his notebook from his pocket. 'I wrote down what I was thinking. Shall I read it to you?'

'You were *writing!*' Paul shook his head in disgust. 'Who

wants to hear anything you'd write? Not me, for one . . .
You were writing while Butch was fighting a bull. I reckon
I've heard the lot after that.'

Gussie had been quiet until then. 'Read it, Adrian.'

Paul turned on his sister with anger. 'Whose side are you
on?'

'There shouldn't be any sides.' It was hard for Gussie to be
blunt with Paul. 'We've got to stick together, haven't we?'

'Adrian should have thought of that before he ran away.
He hasn't even said he's sorry.'

'You weren't here, Paul, when it happened. Adrian's sorry.
We all know he's sorry.'

Paul blew his nose loudly and turned away, and mixed up
with his genuine disgust was a feeling of injury. He had done
all the work and Adrian had done all the dodging, but one
wouldn't think so. One would almost think it was the other
way round.

'Are we all here?' said Adrian.

'All except Harvey,' said Frances.

'Harvey!' yelled Adrian, 'you're wanted.'

They waited for the little chap and Adrian was searching
his mind, almost frantically, for the words to begin with. How
was he to start? Perhaps they were being kinder than he had
expected, but it wouldn't take much to change the climate,
because Paul was against him and Paul was the stronger.

Harvey came in with Buzz tucked firmly under his arm.
'What's on? Somethin' to eat?'

They ignored him and Harvey pouted and sat on the floor
and stroked his dog.

Adrian took a deep breath, because he hadn't found the
words he wanted. He opened his notebook and his hands were
trembling, but still he couldn't think of the words he wanted.

'Well?' mocked Paul. 'What are we waiting for? A fan-
fare?'

Adrian felt the magic of his moment slipping away, so plunged straight into it, reading from the book, without those words of introduction that he had been unable to find.

'Harvey and Butch – light a big fire for a signal and burn on it all decaying food and rotting material.

'Paul – trap or shoot the bull and any other dangerous animals. Find Mr Tobias. Bring Rickard's horse and cart.

'Adrian – find Miss Godwin. Disconnect all electricity wires. Rig power-line for wireless. Start power-plant and signal for help. Miss Godwin's found, so I don't have to do the first part.

'Frances – look after Miss Godwin. Move into the best house you can find with proper facilities for washing and heating and cooking and sleeping and ensure a safe water supply.

'Gussie and Maisie – feed and count all tame animals, fowls and pet birds.

'Everyone, except Adrian and Paul, when their other jobs are finished, will clean up the main street, salvage people's property and carry rubbish to signal-fire.

'Adrian and Paul – as soon as possible are to set out for Fiddler's Crossing with torches and food for two days.

'Signals. Everyone will carry a whistle. In an emergency the signal is twelve short blasts, because everyone is bound to hear some of them. On the emergency signal everyone is to return at once to the shop. The ordinary recall signal for meals or new orders is six long blasts on the whistle.

'Everyone is to sign at the bottom of the page and obey these orders.'

Adrian looked up nervously and they were staring at him, even Paul, and he didn't know whether they were going to laugh or sneer.

Gradually they looked to Paul; all heads seemed to turn in his direction, and Adrian was sickening with anxiety. If they were going to laugh he wished they would get on with it. If they were going to sneer why didn't they start?

Paul, in truth, was astonished, yet in a most unusual way immensely relieved. He was relieved because this was a plan that gave them something to do. It was the lead they all had wanted. And he was astonished because it had come from Adrian. And he was bewildered because it was so simple.

'Yes,' he said. 'Why not?'

Adrian's mouth fell open and slowly across his earnest young face spread a wide smile of real happiness.

'Gee!' he said.

Paul had more to say. 'I want to put it to the vote, the way they do at the town committee meeting. All in favour of Adrian's plan, raise their hands.'

All raised their hands, and Maisie suddenly shouted, 'Three cheers for Adrian!'

They cheered him and Adrian blushed and Frances said, 'The grown-ups were wrong. We'll live all right. Nothing can beat us now.'

'Righto,' said Paul. 'Put the book on the counter, Adrian. We'll all read our orders again and sign it.'

CHAPTER FIFTEEN

The Valiant Children

SLOWLY the fog went up, drifting, eddying, moving like a cloudy impurity suspended in a fluid, always rising as if seeking an invisible surface, until it seemed to be motionless overhead, until it lay above Hills End, six or seven hundred feet up, and rested against the mountain-sides. It still concealed the upper slopes from view, but it granted to the children of Hills End the mercy of visibility. They could see. They seemed to be working and living in an isolated bubble of clear air, safe, encompassed in every direction by forest or earth or impenetrable fog. There seemed to be something special about it, as though they truly were the last people left on earth and the earth were preparing to help them.

There were a number of things that had to be done before they could start their duties, but they were done promptly because they were anxious to begin. Each person seemed to have a real importance, and it was surprising how anxious they all were to prove themselves. Adrian had fitted each task so perfectly to the person or persons from whom it was demanded that it was obvious, particularly to Frances, that his idea was not half-baked. It was mature, almost as though a man were directing it.

Adrian even organized those things that had to be done first. The fat volume he had brought down from the house was called *The Home Doctor* and from its instructions he directed Frances to bind up Butch's feet and fit him with strong boots, then to clean and dress with germicidal ointment the deep scratch that a nail or a wood splinter had scored across his back. He confirmed that all they could do for Miss Godwin was to keep her warm, to allow her to sleep on, and to give her nourishing fluids if she recovered consciousness. The fact remained that she needed a doctor desperately.

Adrian ordered Maisie and Gussie and Harvey to return to the area of the schoolhouse and recover every portion of Miss Godwin's manuscript that they could possibly find. He told Paul how to clean the rifle and pull it through and how to reload it, and from one of his pockets produced the tools and the cartridges. He then collected Mr Matheson's tool-bag from beneath the shop counter, checked its contents, and had set off downhill towards the engine shed into the flood, before they fully realized he had gone.

Paul, for a minute or two, found himself alone with Frances. There were not any words to fit the situation. All they had for each other was a smile of real confidence and real hope. He took up his rifle and walked firmly to the window, like a man.

'Take care,' she called.

He grinned and legged through and strode away up the road, towards the hills.

It must have been after three o'clock before Paul came back into town, riding bareback on Rickard's horse, riding slowly because it was not the habit of the wise old horse to exert himself. At his heels, plodding just as leisurely, just as slowly, was Rickard's old red collie dog. Paul came back with his several tasks completed and before him he could see the devastated face of Hills End slowly changing.

In reality, it was little, because the strength of the children was limited and the task would have daunted a hundred men. From the vacant land adjoining the shop an immense column of dirty smoke billowed towards the fog line. He could hear voices and clatter. He could see along the street, at intervals of fifty or sixty yards the still remaining spoil of the storm, small but orderly stacks of salvaged timber and roofing iron and neat little piles of broken plaster and cement sheet. He saw Gussie dragging a huge piece of wood from the wreckage of the hall with the tenacity of a terrier and Butch, poor old Butch with a wheelbarrow, panting and struggling with a load of rubbish towards the main fire. He could hear the crack of an axe-blade from higher up, where many smaller fires added their smoke to the air.

Something compelled Paul to stop the horse before his friends saw him. For those few moments he seemed to be detached; he enjoyed the brief privilege of seeing himself and his friends as others might have seen them, and he could do nothing but thrill with a rueful pride. A few hours before he had been so dreadfully frightened. The future had looked so black and so full of despair. It still had its shadows, but it was different. Then, they had seemed so helpless, so overwhelmed by dangers and difficulties, so well on the way to fulfilling his father's prophecy that kids would go under if they had to look after themselves.

There was Maisie now, staggering towards the fire with a great armful of newspapers and magazines that had been ruined by water, that probably she had scraped out of ditches or untangled from shrubs or peeled from muddy paths; and there was Gussie dumping her piece of timber on a near-by stack and straightening it neatly; and from Campbell's house, on the hill behind the site of the hall, another column of smoke was rising from a chimney. There, it seemed, Frances must have found the facilities for washing and heating and cooking and sleeping and the safe water supply that Adrian had ordered.

Where was Adrian?

Paul glanced down to the flats and saw that during his absence the receding waters of the river had retreated beyond the mill. The engine shed, once standing in a courtyard of wood shavings, now looked like a miniature Noah's ark stranded in a lake of mud and half-sunken debris. Leaning against the big pole beside the engine shed was an extension ladder, and at the top of the pole, looped over the crossbeams, were many coils of wire that Adrian had salvaged from fallen power-lines, but neither of the engines in the shed was beating. In that respect, at least, Adrian seemed to have failed.

Suddenly a dog was barking. It was Maisie's boxer and it brought an immediate response from Rickard's collie and an excited yell from Gussie, 'Paul's back!'

They raced towards him, Gussie, Maisie, and Butch, and Paul slid from the horse to the ground just in time to catch the bumble-footed Gussie as she tripped. He set her back on her feet and she was bright-eyed and flushed.

'Oh, Paul,' she panted, 'is everything all right?'

His smile wasn't a real smile. 'The bull's out of the way, thanks to Butch, I guess.'

Butch whistled. 'Was he dead? Did I kill him?'

'Far from it. Very far from dead, but he'd gone home and I lured him into the milking yard.'

'Lured him?' squealed Gussie.

Paul wrinkled his brow, perhaps in modesty, but perhaps in respect to the truth. 'Well – if a fella runs helter-skelter and a bull roars down like an express train, I guess it's luring – in a sort of way. Anyhow, he's in the milking yard and the gate's barred. He won't get out in a hurry. But I guess he needs a vet, poor brute. I reckon I jumped ten feet clear in the air to get out of that yard.'

Gussie shivered and Maisie said, 'Did you see any sign of Mr Tobias?'

'I got the old horse,' Paul said, 'and went looking for the cows. Found two of them with their calves. Must have been a mile downstream. Couldn't find the rest anywhere. I suppose they've gone bush or been drowned. Couldn't bring the cart. Didn't know how to get the horse into the shafts. Fancy living in the country all my life and still can't harness a horse. Golly, I got into a tangle! Where's Adrian?'

Gussie glanced at Maisie, and Butch said, 'Gone.'

Paul's heart jumped in a peculiar way. 'Not – he didn't electrocute himself?'

'Of course not,' snorted Gussie. 'Don't be silly. What on earth would make you think a thing like that? He's gone to the crossing.'

'By himself?'

Maisie nodded. 'He had a good lunch and then he went. He's got plenty of food and a good torch and spare batteries. He said he had thought things over. That it was best for you to stay here and look after us.'

Paul wondered about that. He wasn't too sure. 'I see,' he said. 'But two days by himself – Adrian, of all people!'

'He said he didn't want you to go after him.'

'Did he?'

'He couldn't fix up the power-plant, Paul. He says it'll take an engineer. He said both engines had run out of fuel and he couldn't understand why. How could both engines run out of fuel? That's what he said. He said perhaps you'd like to have a look at them.'

'Me? Golly, I don't know anything about engines.'

'But he fixed the wireless up,' said Gussie. 'He brought it down to the shop and rigged up the power from car batteries. He's got ten of them on the floor of the shop, all wired up to give a hundred and twenty volts. Adrian says all you need is a hundred and ten volts, but a hundred and twenty will make sure.'

Paul frowned. 'Where do I fit in? I don't know anything about volts. I can't work a wireless. Adrian's learnt all these things from his dad. My dad doesn't know anything about electricity.'

'Everything is ready for you,' explained Maisie. 'All you've got to do is turn the switch and talk into the microphone. Adrian tried but couldn't raise anyone. He said it might be better later in the day or after dark. He says if you've got any spare time it might help if you make the aerial longer.'

'That's right,' said Butch. 'I'll help.'

'Paul,' Maisie said, 'did you see anything of Mr Tobias?'

'Perhaps I'd better get on with this wireless straight away. We've got to get a doctor in, haven't we, for Miss Godwin?'

'That's why Adrian's gone,' explained Gussie. 'He said there might be a doctor waiting at the bridge, there might be a lot of people there, unable to get across, but with someone on this side to catch it they might be able to throw a rope or something.'

Paul gave the reins of the horse to Butch. 'Tie him up somewhere, Butch. I'll have a look at the wireless ... Where's Harvey, anyway?'

'Up the hill with an axe, having the time of his life ... But you still haven't answered Maisie's question, Paul, about Mr Tobias.'

Paul tried to ignore it again, but realized they had to know sooner or later. 'He's here,' he sighed, 'up on Rickard's place in a ditch. Drowned.'

Gussie had been going to tell Paul about her poor little goldfish that she had found dead in the midst of her broken aquarium, but it didn't seem to be important any more.

Adrian had dressed in his stoutest clothes and put on his hardest-wearing boots. Round each trouser-leg he had added a sugar-bag, bound firmly into place. He carried a tomahawk in his belt and a stout stick in his gloved hand, wore his father's flying helmet to protect his head, and carried on his back a haversack filled with food, first-aid supplies, torch batteries, and a large square of waterproof sheeting. Adrian had tackled it systematically, but it would be far from the truth to say that he had tackled it without anxiety.

Adrian couldn't change his nature. With all the will in the world he couldn't turn himself into what he considered to be a hero. He hurried along the road, or through the bush where the road was impassable, as fast as he could go, not so much because he was in a hurry, but because of a half-formed notion that the faster he went the longer the daylight would last. It was a silly idea that simply wouldn't stand up to reality, but he couldn't slow down. This compulsion that was fear of the night drove him on and on. He didn't seem to realize that the faster he went the farther he placed himself away from his friends. The only thing wrong with Adrian's idea was Adrian himself.

Unfortunately, he had dressed not for speed, but for protection. Soon he was wet with perspiration and he had to peel off his gloves and then his flying helmet and wipe his brow and mop his neck again and again. The haversack was heavy and thudded against his back and shortened his breath. The shoulder straps bore down and hurt him and seemed to rub against the bone and he had to grit his teeth to bear it. And bear it he would, the soreness and the shortness of breath and the stitch in his side, because he would not pause, he would not rest, he had to hurry on to hold back the night. It might have been hours away, but he dreaded the night, because that fog hanging up there above the trees would ooze down again and turn all outlines into the forms of ghosts and all sounds into the cries and murmurs of ghosts.

In truth, Adrian had not changed his mind. In truth, he had never intended that Paul should accompany him. He had resolved to do this alone. He had sworn to himself that he would drive himself until he dropped. He believed he had seen himself for what he was and he would not rest until he had won his honour. He didn't know how like his father he was. His father didn't know either. There were many occasions when Ben Fiddler had little regard for his son. Ben didn't know his son any better than the boy knew himself.

The ruined road wound on beside the roaring river, higher into the mountains and deeper into them and Adrian was climbing towards the fog. It didn't need to come down. He didn't have to wait for night to press it down. He climbed into it and it drifted round him and through the trees and the air became cold again and damp and harsh to breathe. He had to force himself on, against his nature, against the fears and the shapes created by his imagination.

Suddenly, he stopped short, gasping with fright.

He scarcely knew what it was that came out of the fog and grabbed him, except that it was a man, a wild-looking man who clutched him and panted against him and repeated his name over and over again. 'Adrian. Adrian. Adrian.'

So intense had been the boy's concentration, so fierce his fight against his fears, that he didn't understand what had happened until he saw that the wild man was not alone. There were others, just as wild, just as dirty, just as unrecognizable as his own father.

'*Dad!*'

Adrian shouted it to the heavens and flung his arms round

his father and held on fiercely until he almost crushed the breath out of his own body. There never had been a moment more wonderful. They were saved. Men had come back into the world.

'Oh, dad . . .'

He still clung to his father with his face buried in the wet and tattered fabric of the big man's coat, trembling, but not crying, and proud, so proud. He didn't see his father's emotion; didn't see the fear in the faces of the other men.

'Son.'

Adrian straightened himself, too breathless to speak. He hadn't realized that the other men were so close, Mr Mace, Mr McLeod, Maisie's dad, Butch's dad and Harvey's. The fathers were there. They'd all come back and more were with them.

'Why are you alone, son? Where are the other children?'

Adrian squared his shoulders with his pride, because he could see that all these men were almost beside themselves with anxiety. They thought their children were dead. They were blaming themselves because they had left their children behind. Adrian knew that they had lacked faith in their children. He could see it in their haggard faces, in their very wildness, in the bruises and scratches and bloodstains and exhaustion that they had inflicted upon themselves in their desperate journey from somewhere far away.

Adrian grinned. 'We're all well,' he said, 'every single one of us.'

Adrian was astonished because he saw tears in the eyes of men. He had never seen men cry. He had never imagined that they could, and he felt the pressure of his father's hand bearing down on his shoulder forcing him to kneel.

'Let us pray,' said Ben.

They all knelt, but Big Ben said nothing. For a minute he was silent and then uttered his only word, 'Amen.'

Adrian looked up and the men were rising and his father said, 'Righto, chaps. We'll be on our way. Give me that haversack, lad . . . You see before you, son, men of little faith. We should have known better. We should have known that Frank Tobias and Miss Godwin – and the Good Lord – would take care of you all.'

Adrian almost corrected his father, but something held him back. The denial was on the tip of his tongue but he stifled it. Let them find out for themselves. Let them see. Let them learn.

'What were you about to say, son?'

Adrian shook his head. 'Nothing.'

'If there's anything we should know,' said Mr Mace sharply, 'let us know now, Adrian. Don't tell us our children are safe if they're not.'

'We *are* safe. The *children* are all right.'

Big Ben's hand was still tight on Adrian's shoulder. 'What's the trouble, son? Out with it!'

Adrian's confidence in himself began to totter. He was back in the world of men. Back in the world of questions and answers and orders and impatient adult minds. For a while he had felt like a man himself. Every second now he was feeling more and more like a boy.

'What are you doing here, son? Why aren't you with the others?'

'I was going for a doctor,' he stammered.

'Doctor!' Big Ben's hand tightened like a vice. '*Who* wants a doctor?'

'Miss – Miss Godwin. She's sick. She's terribly sick.'

'Well, what's wrong with Frank Tobias? What does he mean by sending a boy?'

'Let me go,' stammered Adrian. 'You're hurting me.'

'Yes, ease up, Ben. Don't frighten the lad.'

Big Ben dropped his hand and Mr Mace said gently, 'Forgive your father. He's had a harder time than any of us. He's carried the guilt on his own conscience, though we told him he shouldn't.'

Big Ben sighed. 'I'm sorry.'

'If you were going to tell your father anything, tell him now. If we do have to go for a doctor, Adrian, it's far better that one or two of us should go from here. We're too tired to walk the extra distance home and back again if it can be avoided. You understand?'

Adrian nodded and started his explanation in a level enough voice, but became more breathless, more strained, as he continued. 'We want the doctor for Miss Godwin. We think she might die. And Mr Tobias didn't send me because he couldn't. You can't blame him for anything because we haven't seen him. We think he's dead. And the town's a wreck. It's almost wiped out. It's awful. But you know, don't you? You sent the aeroplane.'

They didn't reply immediately, neither Big Ben nor Mr Mace. It was Harvey's father who finally spoke, 'I find myself wondering what these kids have been through. Let's go, huh?'

'In a moment,' said Big Ben. 'No, son. We didn't send the aeroplane. The only warning we've had is what we've seen. The farther we've come the worse it has been. If it hadn't been for that we could not have crossed the gorge. If it hadn't been for landslides and fallen trees we would not have been able to cross to this side . . . Aeroplane. That's interesting. If they know about us there'll be others coming behind, and if the police at Stanley have got the sense I give them credit for there'll be a doctor . . . What about it, you two?'

He sought out, with a quick glance, a couple of young men. 'Yes, Maurie and Norm. Your bones are the youngest and you haven't any kids to worry about. Would you mind, terribly, going back and waiting at the Crossing? Escort them through. Show them the way. May be a day's wait.'

'Of course we don't mind, sir. Do we, Norm? That's what we're here for. But what has Adrian got in his haversack? Anything to eat?'

Adrian nodded. 'Take it.'

They took it, and Big Ben said. 'Thanks, chaps. Good luck to you . . . And, as for the rest of us, we'd better be getting home.'

Adrian noted how aged his father looked. Perhaps it was the grime or his unshaven face. Perhaps it was something else. And it was. If Big Ben had lost his town and his good mate Frank Tobias, he'd almost lost his own life.

At twenty minutes past five o'clock eight men and a boy plodded across the clearing that had brought to the children, a day before, their first view of the ruins of Hills End. It brought now to the men almost the same view, almost the same shock. Layers of fog drifted here and there and smoke from a dozen fires hung low, but nothing could hide the awful havoc. It was too much for Ben Fiddler. He couldn't look upon it. His empire in the forest was dead.

The other men, no matter how shocked they were, no matter how deeply wounded by the loss of their homes and their jobs, were still apart from him. Ben's loss was more than the loss of material things. It was the loss of his dream. It was the loss of the way of life he had built with his own brain and his own hands. So great was his loss, so terrible was the destruction, that surely it must be a judgement from God. He had believed he was a good man, but he could not have been. This was so savage, so final. He was ruined.

Big Ben heard the voices of men who worked for him, good chaps all, expressing their sorrow, thinking of him even when they had lost so much themselves, and suddenly, cruelly it was, the voices were lost in the shrill, short blasts of a whistle.

It was Adrian, blowing with all his might, and Big Ben was so outraged he could have struck the boy down.

'Stop that!' he bellowed.

Adrian lowered his whistle, startled, not understanding. 'But, dad,' he said, 'I was only calling the kids. It's our signal.'

'Signal! Signal! Don't you dare do it again.'

Adrian shrank, frightened by this anger, wondering how he could have forgotten this wrath that so often was in his father. The grown-ups were back all right. It had been tough without them, but a fellow forgot these things. His father was so masterful, so stern, so much like an old-time prophet. It had never been easy to live in his house.

Then he realized that he was alone with his father. The men had gone, perhaps drawn by the distant shouts of the children and the excited barking of the dogs, or perhaps too embarrassed to stay or too impatient to wait on the pleasure of their boss. They had gone and were running, and towards them, from far away, Adrian could see the children running. He envied them somehow. No other father ruled as his father ruled. Adrian was set apart from his friends again. The danger might have passed, but so had a great deal more.

Slowly Adrian pushed his whistle back into his pocket, and somehow it was symbolic. It seemed to signify the putting away of the little bit of dignity he had had, the little bit of bravery, and the adventure of fighting back.

His father started walking down the hill with the hesitant gait of a broken man, and Adrian followed two or three paces behind. He couldn't even feel sorry for his father, because how could anyone feel sorry for such a man?

They met the others at the end of the main street. Little Harvey was sitting like a king on his father's shoulders. Gussie was hugging Mr Mace's arm as though scared to let go. Butch was telling his dad all about the bull. Maisie was holding her father's hand and squeezing it. Paul, just a little apart, was watching Mr Fiddler's approach, was watching Adrian pace miserably behind, and he realized then that he had been hard on his friend. Adrian might have had nicer clothes and a better cricket bat, might have had more of everything, but in the real things he was poor.

'You ought to hear this,' said Butch's dad proudly. 'Young Christopher took on Rickard's bull, bare-handed.'

'Me, too,' squeaked Harvey, 'and Paul. Don't forget Paul.'

Ben Fiddler seemed to dig in his toes. He swayed a little, looked from face to face. He seemed to be ageing in front of their eyes.

'Bull?'

'I told you so,' said Harvey's father. 'These kids have had a time.'

'You didn't tell me anything about a bull, Adrian.'

Adrian shrugged and dropped his eyes.

'Your son,' said Mr Mace, 'was not exactly encouraged to tell us anything.'

That wasn't entirely true, but seemed to be the thing to say. Big Ben ignored it. 'Where's Frances?'

'At Campbell's house,' said Paul, 'looking after Miss Godwin. Mr McLeod has gone on to her. Miss Godwin has taken a little broth.'

'Adrian said she was desperately ill, that she needed a doctor. We've sent men back.'

'She is ill,' snapped Paul, with unusual heat.

Big Ben glanced at the boy and Mr Mace said, 'Be patient, Ben. He's had a shock. He found Frank Tobias, dead.'

Big Ben ran his hand across his brow and passed through the group in silence, and on into the township, with Adrian once more a few paces behind.

Awkwardly, a couple at a time, they followed in a straggling procession, the joy of their reunion dampened and their realization of the destruction becoming stronger at every step.

For a minute or two Ben Fiddler paused at the foot of the terraced hill below his house, and thereafter as he came to each house paused again, until they were standing in the midst of the wreckage of the hall.

'The death of a town,' he said. 'Dead.'

Adrian's voice was very small. 'It's not dead, dad. We're rebuilding already. We've started.'

Big Ben turned his head slowly over the orderly heaps of broken timber and twisted iron, over the scratches in the ground where children had dragged garden rakes, and up to the smoke of the fires. 'What are you burning?' he said sharply. 'How dare you burn? What are you burning?'

'You're a big bully,' Paul yelled.

'Paul!' roared Mr Mace. 'Be quiet. You don't understand.'

'I do understand,' cried Paul. 'We're burning rubbish, that's what. We're cleaning up. We've raked the streets. Cleared the drains. Salvaged hymn-books and Bibles and people's property. Adrian's even tried to start the power-plant. Risked his life cutting wires and dragging them out of the mud. We've had to trap a bull. We've had to find Miss Godwin. We've had to do everything by ourselves. We've looked for the animals and fed them. We've even chased the fowls and caught them. We've fixed up the wireless and called for help. We've cleaned out all the refrigerators and the rotten, stinking meat. We've got a plan and it's Adrian's plan. He organized it. That's what we're doing, and don't you dare say to us "*how dare we do it!*"'

Big Ben Fiddler was white beneath his grime and dirt and a pulse was beating violently in his temple.

'That was quite a speech, boy,' he said coldly, 'but I'll overlook it because you're upset and you don't know what you're saying.'

He turned from the road on to the track up to Campbell's

house, and Adrian followed meekly. Paul's father took him by the collar.

'You're to apologize to Mr Fiddler. At once. Get yourself after him.'

Paul shook himself free. 'I won't apologize. He's a rotten bully. If he thinks the town looks a wreck now he should have seen it before we started.'

'That's right,' said Butch stoutly.

'Keep out of it, Butch,' said Paul, 'it's not your fight.'

'You will apologize, Paul,' ordered Mr Mace. 'Mr Fiddler built this town. It's his life, and you can't understand. You're only a child. Even I can see it's finished. It'd take a year to re-build. Thousands and thousands and thousands of pounds. And while he rebuilds how does he pay his men? What happens to his contracts? Without the mill there's nothing. The roads have gone. The bridge has gone. Do you understand now?'

'I understand that insurance will pay most of it and I wouldn't think much of my father if he couldn't work without wages for a while.'

Butch's dad said quietly, 'Our boys are growing up. Paul, why don't you tell Mr Fiddler that you didn't mean to hurt him, that you do respect him, in spite of what you said?'

Paul looked at his father, and Mr Mace managed to smile back, because in truth he was filled with pride of his son. 'Very well. Will you do that?'

'Yes, dad.'

Gussie took his hand and all headed for the track to Campbell's place, hurrying to overtake Ben Fiddler and Adrian.

Frances had made up a bed for Miss Godwin in the big kitchen of the Campbell home. The house had suffered, as all had suffered, yet the kitchen side had escaped almost unharmed. When they all entered the room was warm and a black iron kettle was boiling on the stove and tea-cups were lined up along the sink. There was the homely smell of eggs and sliced tinned meat frying in a large pan. There was Mr McLeod standing with his daughter at the head of the bed, and Miss Godwin, sitting up, supported by pillows.

Her eyes seemed to be as pale as the rest of her, lost somewhere in the depths of the sunken shadows about them, but she was herself, because there was the kind of smile they had always known. It seemed that she had been waiting for all the men to come and for all the children. She wanted all her children around her.

Adrian felt towards her an outpouring of emotion such as he might have given to his mother, felt a bond towards her that was stronger than ever, perhaps because his father had treated him so badly and so ignorantly. But he felt, too, a deep and painful pang of conscience that he knew he would have to put right. That he had tried and failed as far as his father was concerned mattered a great deal, but this mattered more. He knew she was beckoning him, and he glanced at Paul and both stood beside her bed.

She said thinly, 'I'm so proud of my brave boys and girls. Frances has told me and I'm so proud. You've taught me such a lesson.'

Adrian knew he had to say it, knew he had to say it now. 'Miss Godwin, I told you a lie and I want to put it straight.'

Her smile faded. 'Don't tell me anything that's going to hurt you.'

'I want to tell you. I've got to tell you. I didn't know the paintings were in the cave. It was a big lie.'

Adrian knew that every eye was on him, knew that his father had gasped aloud, but it didn't silence him. Instead he felt a release from something bad, and the freedom from it warmed him through and through. 'It's not right,' he said, 'that the discovery should be called after me. I don't deserve it. It's to be called after you.'

Her eyes had closed, almost tightly, and odd little movements had started flickering round her mouth. For a moment of panic Adrian thought he had said the wrong thing, but slowly her gentle smile began to form again long before she opened her eyes and reached out a hand to Frances.

'No,' she said clearly. 'I've had my reward, in so many ways. Name it instead in honour of the children of Hills End. Let it be known as the "Cave of the Valiant Children", because, good friends, the children have shown us the way.'

Adrian saw then that she wasn't looking at him at all, but looking past him into the eyes of the men, from man to man, deliberately, with an expression that might have been of wisdom, but might even have been a demand. Last of all she came to Ben Fiddler and held his gaze until he was compelled to step forward.

He reached out both hands and drew Adrian into his right arm and Paul into his left. 'Thank you, Miss Godwin,' he said. 'Indeed, they have shown us the way.'